SPOOKED BY A SUSPICION

RISA NYMAN

Hope life's changes bring you joy—

Risa Nyman

Immortal Works LLC
1505 Glenrose Drive
Salt Lake City, Utah 84104
Tel: (385) 202-0116

© 2021 Risa Nyman
https://www.risanyman.com/

Cover Art by Ashley Literski
http://strangedevotion.wixsite.com/strangedesigns

ISBN 978-1-953491-21-3 (Paperback)
ASIN B099QJGT24 (Kindle Edition)

For Brenda, Pam, and Devora who bring joy to my life beyond measure.

PART 1:
HOME IN MILTON

CHAPTER 1

My nostrils twitch. I crank open my eyelids halfway and suck in the aroma that's seeping under my bedroom door. That smell signals this will not be an ordinary morning. In superhero speed, I'm out of bed and pulling on my sweat pants because there's a strict no-boxers-at-the-table rule.

I fly down the stairs. Aha! I knew it! C-buns crowned in white in the middle of the table. I reach over and give one of them a squeeze. Still warm.

"Hey, Mom," I say, about to ask her what's the occasion, when she pivots around from the stove like a ballet dancer. She stuns me with a smile that's almost too large for her face to hold. Oh, yeah, there's going to be some rockin' good news today. Maybe even great news.

"Why are you so happy?" I ask, noticing scrambled eggs, bacon, and OJ that looks fresh squeezed. She's prepared a feast. I snag a bacon strip as I park my butt and crunch down, listening to the crispiness echo in my ears.

"No yoga today?" Mom never misses her Saturday morning class, insisting it decompresses her after a week of studying spreadsheets with endless columns of numbers.

She brings over a bowl of melon chunks and says, "I've got a big announcement. I'm just waiting for Grandpa to come down."

The gears in my head rotate on all the possibilities for best surprise announcement until I get to Harry Potter World in Orlando, and they stop. That's my number one choice, but club seats for a Revolution's soccer game is a close runner-up. The most outstanding news would be seeing Mom flash a winning lottery ticket in my face. We could be millionaires!

Grandpa walks in and pours his coffee before he joins me at the table. "How's my handsome goalie grandson this fine morning?"

"Hungry!" I say.

Mom takes a seat, still wearing that supersized smile.

"Hey, what's with the major breakfast today?" I ask, putting a cinnamon bun on my plate and buttering it. Mom always says no need for added butter, but I totally disagree.

She clangs her fork and knife against the table while making rat-a-tat-tat noises, and says, "Drum roll, please."

Grandpa and I look up at the same time as she announces, "Ted and I are getting married."

What did I just hear? My mouth stops mid-chew.

"Ted's very special," she continues, but her words are losing their form in my ears like a puff of smoke. I'm not listening anymore. How could this happen?

Yes, that guy has been here a lot, but I thought his accounting work must be so complicated it had to spill over into dinnertime. They went to the movies once or twice, but does that mean you have to marry someone? Then she chopped off her long hair, which annoyed me because Dad always complimented her blonde, silky ponytail. Did she do that for Ted? And she did give me the talk about how she hoped to remarry someday, but I assumed someday meant four years from now, when I'm away in college. *Rocky, you're so clueless!*

"And me?" I ask. "Aren't I special?" Yikes, I sound like a whiny baby. I glance at Grandpa, waiting for him to step in and clean up this pile of crap that has landed in our dining room, but his eyes tell a different story. They sparkle in a way usually reserved just for me, his only grandchild.

"I'm so happy for you, Marybeth," he says.

Well, Grandpa, you can have the luxury to be on board with this catastrophe because it isn't your life taking a deep dive into the unknown. Another change in my life might kill me. Okay, that might be an exaggeration, but she's dumped me in a pit of quicksand, and I'm struggling to keep from going under.

Mom says, "You're special, Rocky, in a different way. You're my son. The more you get to know Ted, the more you'll see how wonderful he is."

When she mentions his name, her grin grows even wider in a record-breaking stretch, and her blue eyes shine with silvery specks as if she sprinkled them with glitter. Now that I know her joyful expression isn't predicting anything good for me, I wish she'd tone it down.

"When's this supposed to happen?" I ask, curious how much time I have to pull the plug on her plans.

"No definite date yet," she says.

There's still time.

"Does he have kids?" I need to know everything about him, so I can stop this craziness.

"No. He's never been married before. Also, I asked Ted to come to your game today. He's picking us up at ten thirty. Guess what? He's never attended a soccer game before in his whole life!"

So, in a flash, this guy morphs from client status into about-to-be husband and scores an invite to watch me play.

Kids should only have to have one major change in their lives, and I've already had mine.

CHAPTER 2

Mom's news is an appetite killer and might have ruined cinnamon buns for me for the rest of my life. I leave the kitchen to get ready for the game, but mostly to escape and think.

After I put on my socks and cleats and stuff some soccer gear in my bag, I open my computer to do an Internet search on Ted. How well does Mom know him? He could have a criminal record, or there might be something horrible in his past. It's my duty as the son to discover what might lurk beneath his strange face.

I boot up my computer, type in *Ted* and stop, aware that Mom is planning to marry a guy, and I don't even know his last name. So much for googling him. I close the laptop and go back downstairs.

At ten thirty sharp, Ted arrives. I suspect that his punctuality is part of a before-the-wedding act, which will disappear right after they're married. Mom's brain must not be operating on full power, and it's up to me to protect her from this looming disaster. I'll have to find out his last name as soon as possible.

Mom gets into the front passenger seat. Ted opens the trunk, and I stow my bag.

He says, "So your mom told you our wonderful news. Exciting, isn't it?"

"Exciting like an earthquake," I reply, feeling no obligation to protect him from my opinion about Mom's announcement.

I watch his smile vanish into the asphalt of the driveway. Victorious, I climb into the back seat.

All the way to Skyline Field, the dude can't stop blabbering about going to his first soccer game ever. Ted says, "It's difficult to conceive of a game that's all about the ball, yet the players are penalized for touching it. It goes against all instinct. Balls are meant to be thrown. It's basic; toss a ball to a baby, and they will automatically throw it back to you."

This guy is a big durk, my new word for dumb jerk. He has no kids and is pretending to be some kind of expert on baby behavior. My buddy Max with his new baby brother probably knows more about babies than this bozo. And I don't see it as my job to educate this soccer dummy that I, as the goalie, can touch the ball.

He continues to show off his soccer ignorance with a flood of questions, and Mom just sits there, allowing Ted to monopolize the conversation. I wish I had brought my headphones to block out his jabber.

He asks, "Rocky, how did you decide to play goalie?"

Boy, he is ignorant. You don't decide something like that. The position finds you. Dad was a high school and college soccer superstar, and by the time I was six, he claimed I was born to guard the goal. I'm not sharing that with Ted because it's way too personal, so I answer, "Just did," and pray he has exhausted his soccer talk.

As soon as he parks, I grab my bag and head for the field. After putting on my red goalie shirt, I shove my hands into well-worn goalie gloves, which no longer dazzle with their neon yellow brightness. I doubt I will ever retire them, because they were the last present Dad gave me. Their price tag ticked Mom off, and she scolded Dad for another of his many extravagances, but she let me keep them.

The coach sends us onto the field to warm up. Max retrieves balls for me while the other guys practice their kicking.

Then Max says, "Hey, Rocky, who's the dude with your mom?"

Without thinking, my eyes zoom up to the bleachers, but I drop them just as fast, regretting I looked and promise myself not to repeat that during the game. Mom sitting in the stands with a man who isn't Dad or Grandpa is vomit-worthy.

"A client of hers," I reply and turn away as I sense my face reddening from the heat rising in my chest. I run behind the net to scoop up wayward balls so Max can't see my embarrassment. I don't want to have to answer more questions about Ted.

On the way to the huddle, Max whispers, "A client? Are you sure? He can't stop staring at your mom."

Max and I are tight like my last year's cleats, but still I narrow my eyes until they join together in a "back off" message. I don't want to talk about this.

The team is called to forms circle, and Max leads the before-game chant as we all put our hands into the center. We break and charge onto the field, ready for the Lincoln Lions.

The whistle blows. I take a couple of deep breaths like my counselor showed me after Dad died to calm my stress and refocus on the game. The first half ends with the score still zero to zero. All the shots coming at me were a mile away from the goal.

During halftime, I down a bottle of sports drink and snatch a towel to mop the sweat off. Coach Taylor gives us his standard pep talk and ends with a stern warning: "Do not let up on them. Lincoln has a reputation for second-half fierceness. Stay alert."

As I run back onto the field, I stick to my promise not to look up at Mom and Ted, which would probably make me barf all over the ball.

The Lincoln Lions race out pumped up, just like Coach said they'd be. They bombard me with random shots and misguided passes. For the first ten minutes, I hold them off, but it's rough. Also, Coach sidelined Marco, our star defenseman, with a pulled hamstring, and the backup guy is less than stellar. Without great defenders, this game, any game, rides on the goalie's shoulders.

There's another rush at me from the Lincoln offense. I step out in front of the goal, preparing for the block. The opponent puts his foot on top of the ball to position it for the kick.

At that precise second, Ted's distinct cackle-voice booms, "Go to your left, Rocky. To the left!" This guy, who's never been to a soccer game in his life, is trying to coach me. Un-be-liev-able.

I see the angle and dive to the right to block, stretching my arms to make the stop, as the ball sails into the goal on the far-left side. No way that could happen. I got played like a rookie goalie, and yet somehow Ted knew which way the ball was headed. How is that possible? We lose the game one to zero.

When it's over, Max pats me on the back as I walk off the field. Tony, our star striker, pinches his nose to let me know that play was a stinker. He's right. I blew it. Coach will have something to say about that.

I meet Mom and Ted at the car. He takes my bag and tosses it into the trunk, saying, "Good game."

"You're wrong," I snap back. A loss always stings. I wait for him to ask why I didn't go left when he told me to, but he doesn't mention it, so neither do I.

Mom tries to cheer me up. "Don't be too upset, Rocky. That was like a one in a million shot. No way any goalie could've stopped it."

I don't reply, because there's nothing to say.

Mom leans toward Ted, trying to be super quiet, but I hear every word. "Sometimes he doesn't like to talk after a game," she whispers to him. "It takes time for him to process."

I'm processing all right. I'm processing whether this is really Ted's first game as he claims, or a giant hoax. Perhaps he's a con man, and he convinced Mom to marry him under false pretenses. I think that is a crime.

How do we know we can trust him?

CHAPTER 3

I snag a towel from the linen closet and head for the shower, pausing by the mirror. My hair is matted down from dried-up soccer-game sweat, which works like gel but with a sour smell. In the shower, I pour on a ton of body wash and scrub at my arms and legs with a furor, as if I can clean up the sick sensation Mom's wedding plans have left me with. If I could, I'd roll back this morning and wake up to a boring, normal, uneventful breakfast of cereal.

I dress and go downstairs to ask Grandpa if he knows Ted's last name. On my way to the den, I spot Ted's phone and wallet with his keys on top of the kitchen counter. For the first time today, I catch a break. Before I check inside his wallet, I scout out everyone's whereabouts to make sure the coast is clear.

Mom and Ted are sitting in the backyard, and Grandpa is deep into his newspaper. Perfect. Even though I have excellent snooping skills, my nerves sting and the hairs on my arms stand at attention. Adrenaline pumps through my veins as if they're NASCAR tracks. Do real criminals, and I do not consider myself a criminal, ever get used to doing stuff like this?

I take his license out. His full name is Theodore Duddeldorf. OMG poor guy to be saddled with a hilarious name like that. Then it occurs to me that Mom might become Ms. Duddeldorf. No one would know she's my mother if she uses that name. It would be like she and Ted are on the same team, and I don't belong to her anymore.

Then to make this a hundred times worse, if that's even possible, his address is in East Milton. I'm sure as heck not moving to the other side of town. We've been living with Grandpa for a year, and I've adjusted to sleeping in Mom's old room with its pink walls and white lace curtains. She promised to redo it for me but never got around to it. Living in East Milton would mean becoming a bus kid and not being able to walk to my friends' houses. I'd lose the tiny sliver of freedom I now have.

There's a photo behind the license, and although I was hunting only for his name, I can't resist the urge to dig deeper and pull it out. It's a picture of Ted with a woman who isn't Mom and two little smiley kids. Ted has his arm around her, and they both look happy. Even at thirteen, I know keeping a picture of yourself with another woman when you're planning to marry someone else is bad business. And he told Mom he didn't have kids. The boy in the photo kinda resembles him. Strike one, Ted.

Before I return the picture, I turn it over and read the words *Ted and Jeanie* with a recent date. Very suspicious.

I dash up to my room and boot up my computer to google him. While I'm waiting for the apple to appear, Mom and Ted's laughing voices rise up through the vent so I know they're in the kitchen. Suddenly they go quiet. Did I forget to put his keys back on top of his wallet like how I found them? What if they discover I was snooping? I give myself a virtual smack on the side of the head for such a rookie mistake.

Olive, my sort of girlfriend and partner in all detective

matters, will be disappointed if I get caught for a stupid mistake. Last year the two of us did brilliant investigation work trying to unlock Mom's secret about how Dad died. Olive is a solver of mysteries. No one's mind is sharper. The rest of us are mere mortals compared to her.

I should come up with a plausible explanation about the keys, in case they question me. I could say I was carrying a couple of boxes of cereal to make my combo bowl and dropped them on the counter, knocking over the keys. At least I know I was careful to put the license and photo back in the exact way I found them. I'm sure of that.

I return to my search on the computer and remind myself to wipe the computer's history when I'm finished because Mom has rights to check my computer until I turn sixteen.

Bingo! Ted has a construction company that renovates houses. There's some before and after photos on his website of houses about a hundred years old. Then, there's a link offering to get a background check on him. This is exactly what I need, but unfortunately, when I click on the link, I discover that website charges a fee. I can just picture my convo with Mom when I ask to use her credit card.

"For what?" she'd ask.

"Oh, nothing important, just thought I'd check Ted's criminal history." I smile at that ridiculous exchange, but there's nothing funny about any of this. Maybe I should go to the police station and ask them to do a search for him in their records. I'm going to run that by Olive. She'll know if it's an okay plan. I text her, hoping she's on her A game.

Me: Awful news.

Olive: What now? You're like a magnet for trouble.

Me: Mom getting married.

Olive: I love weddings. Fun. Can I come? She adds a lot of

emojis—a wedding cake, champagne glasses, a diamond ring, and a man and woman with a heart between them.

Me: NO! NOT FUN. I have to stop this.

Olive: Why?

Me: What if he has a criminal record or another wife somewhere?

Olive: Ha. Ha. I doubt that. Get real, Rocket Man.

Me: Aren't you supposed to date for at least two years before you get married?

Olive: Not sure there are rules about that.

Me: We've got to do something.

Olive: We???????

Me: This is a monstrous mistake. They might make me move so I'd have to take the bus to school.

Olive: Okay, call me. NOW!

Her photo pops up on my phone when I press her number. She doesn't even waste a moment on "Hi."

"Calm down," she says. "You need evidence if you want to convince her this guy isn't good."

"How do I get that?"

"Start a list of everything strange about him. When the time is right, you will present your list to your mom so she won't go through with this marriage."

"Good idea."

"You'll be like a lawyer preparing a case. This might be excellent training for law school. There are lawyers who play soccer, you know."

"Hilarious. I'm on it. Got to go."

I retrieve a notebook from my nightstand and turn to an empty page. I write on the top in all caps:

REASONS NOT TO MARRY TED

1. Does Mom know this guy, except for doing his taxes?

She should do a background check on him and find out if he has ever been in jail. Did he abandon some kids? Will there be new "grandparents" who insist on getting involved in my life?

2. His pointy beard and bushy eyebrows, which are in continual motion.

Mom would probably dismiss comments about his appearance as unkind, but someone should point out she's planning to marry the weirdest-looking guy in Milton.

That dark little triangle of hair under Ted's lip looks like he copied it off a mask of the devil and those eyebrows of his need to be controlled.

3. Gives unwanted soccer advice.

I put down the notebook, transferring my thoughts to paper is like opening a pressure valve in my head. I'm sure I can fill as many pages as it takes to get Mom to give Ted the boot.

There are three light knocks on my door, which isn't Mom's usual ritual, and Grandpa doesn't do the stairs so much since his hip problem, so the only possibility is Ted. I stash my notebook between my mattress and the wall for security.

After another knock, I say, "Come in."

Ted opens the door and stands on the threshold as if he's waiting for an invitation to enter my territory. I would love to leave him hanging there, but I'm curious about this intrusion, so I say, "You can come in. Do you want something?"

"This is for you, pal." He presents me with a blue suitcase on wheels with a bow on top. "The salesman in the store told me the New England Revolution players use this model on their road trips." He's so pleased that his eyebrows can't stop moving up and down.

Number one, I am not your *pal*, and number two, a suitcase is a peculiar present. There are a million things he could give me that would make more sense, like a new video controller.

"Why do I need a suitcase?" I ask.

"Maybe you'll take a trip soon," he says. Didn't this bonehead ever look in the mirror? The goofy-devil combo makes him resemble the Joker's silly twin.

"I'm not taking any trips," I reply, "but thanks." Mom would kill me if I didn't thank someone for a gift.

I observe Ted checking out my room, and his eyes settling on a photo of Dad with me on his shoulders.

He says, "Sometimes your expression is just like your da—" He doesn't finish his sentence.

"Huh?" Was he going to say I look like Dad? I do not. Dad is dark, and I'm blond and blue-eyed like Mom. I even have the same nose she does, not Dad's big beak that he'd always pretend to honk like a giant goose.

"I mean you resemble your dad in that photo," he says, and his eyebrows stop moving as if he applied the brakes. They are frozen in fright.

"I don't look like him."

"Oh, my mistake. Your mom's waiting for me." He dashes out as if the room just caught fire.

I stare at the suitcase. Is it booby-trapped? Maybe there's a bomb inside, but then again, I'm always being accused of having too much imagination. Okay, no bomb, but a couple of scorpions? I dig around in the bottom of my closet for thick winter gloves for protection and hold a pillow in front of me as a makeshift shield. Then I unzip the suitcase.

Whew! Empty. But I still don't trust him. This present

might be his way of lulling me into lowering my guard for some disaster about to come.

I pull out my notebook and add another entry to my anti-Ted list.

4. The suitcase.

CHAPTER 4

The next day after a restless night of wedding nightmares, it takes all my strength to push open Tucker Middle's heavy green doors and hike up to my third-floor homeroom. I'm exhausted. I take my seat in the back row. Marco swings around and says, "Hey, bro, tough game yesterday."

The soccer game seems like ages ago, but before I reply, Ms. Meller claps us into silence and calls our attention to the whiteboard which has the list of dates for eighth-grade graduation rehearsals. Then she reminds us this is an assembly day, so no first-period class.

Rats! No math today after I wasted an hour last night letting the Pythagorean theorem slurp up my brain juices. Instead I could've drowned in a video game marathon to distract me from my Ted problem.

When homeroom ends, I make my way to the auditorium and scan the room for Olive, whose head rises above the others. She could be a star basketball player, but she runs cross-country just to confuse people. She claims she's taller than me, but we're about the same. I spot her long, dark ponytail and make my way to her row. As usual, she's saved seats for me and Madison, her BFF, who sits in front of me in homeroom.

Max jogs up, and Madison winks at him as we push into the

row. He doesn't respond. I want to kick him in the shins and say, "Wake up, man, a girl winked at you. Don't be a doofus."

We sit, and I get a whiff of his sour odor. "Ooo, dude, not again."

"Baby barf," Max explains, as if I didn't recognize his fragrant scent. "My new brother is marking me as his territory."

"That baby has it in for you," I say.

"The feeling is mutual, except I don't throw up on him or pee all over his shirt whenever I can."

Olive puts on her fake, giggly voice and says, "Sammy is trés adorable."

Max replies, "That's typical of someone who doesn't live with the whims of a baby, sometimes crying, always hungry, and smelly in one way or another."

Max's recent transition from only child status to big brother at age thirteen has been bumpy. I know how that feels, because I'm a certified expert in family changes. My life was thrown against the wall in a gruesome splatter when Dad died, and now Mom has dropped a new bomb into my life.

Olive leans in toward me until our heads almost touch, whispering in my ear, "So did you start your list?"

"Yup, but I have a backup plan, too."

"And?"

"Tell you later."

"Wake me when this assembly is history," Max says and slumps in his seat.

"Me too," I say and slouch down.

Max asks, "What's your excuse? You don't have a crying baby in the room next to you."

"Miserable night. I need to zone out," I say, closing my eyes as the three teacher-claps warn us that there's no more talking.

Tucker Middle School assemblies are routine and boring. They happen almost once a month when the principal, a teacher, or a coach hands out certificates like they're passing out Halloween candy. Everyone gets something. We have assemblies for Fall Sports Awards, Academic Achievement, Attendance Stars, Standout Leaders, and whatever else they can dream up. You can't get through a school year here without picking up at least one certificate, even if it's only for "most improved" or "most conscientious." Those categories are their attempt at a creative approach for kids who excel at nothing.

My eyelids close until something jabs my shoulder nonstop. Olive gushes, "Hey, it's you, Rocky. You've hit the jackpot. Fire your jets and get up there to find out what you've won!" She makes it sound as if I've been called on stage for a quiz show.

I lift my eyes, and Ms. Rotterdam, my English teacher, is at the podium, staring straight at me. She almost swallows the mike as she booms out, "Rocky Casson."

I had no clue I was up for anything at the Humanities Assembly. I push past a bunch of other eighth graders, wishing I hadn't sat in the middle of the row today. Ordinarily, those are the prime seats to prevent you from getting trampled on when other kids are up and down collecting their awards. It's not a great location when you're the person who has to climb over some kid's enormous feet who refuses to move them out of the way. I hope for some miracle to avoid stumbling and landing in someone's lap.

Once I'm in the aisle, I push my hair off my forehead, wishing I had used some gel this morning on my flyaway bangs. I've been on stage before when the Milton Tigers took the middle school soccer division championship, so I know the drill.

I bound up the steps two at a time and move into position next to Dam, as we call Ms. Rotterdam. She lowers her glasses so they hang around her neck and gives me the once-over. Her gray hair is pulled into a bun tight enough to make her eyes pop out of her head. I'm always tempted to offer her a stapler to refasten some loose skin heading south around her chin, but she probably needs a plastic surgeon for that. Still, she's actually a great teacher for an old lady.

Standing up there makes my insides sink to my feet like a falling elevator unable to stop. All this attention upsets my system. I prefer to blend in chameleon-style.

"This year," Ms. Rotterdam announces, "Rocky won the regional award for emerging writers for his short story, *The Pressured Life of a Goalie.*"

Rotterdam gave me an A on that assignment, which I admit I deserved. The story described how bummed I was when we first moved to Milton right after Dad's funeral in the middle of seventh grade, and the goalie position was already taken. I had to play offense, even though goalie is my sweet spot. This year I'm in the net for the Tigers where I belong.

Ms. Rotterdam hands me a certificate. I turn to leave the stage when she puts her arm on mine to stop me. Now what? I'm eager to return to my seat.

She continues in a whisper, "The letter inside is important. Be sure your mom reads it today." Then she roars into the mike, "Congratulations, Rocky, we're very proud of you." She shakes my hand as if she could draw well water from me. My shoulder joint wobbles like a bowl of Jell-O. Then she steers me to the side without easing her grip.

"Don't run off," she instructs. "Hold the certificate near your face and smile." A tall, skinny kid with zits on each cheek, a typical high-school face, snaps our photo. Now I doubly wish I had used gel and didn't wear my Scooby-Doo T-shirt. I'll look like a dork for sure.

Dam says, "Tell your mom they will announce this in the *Milton Chronicle.*"

As I step down from the stage, my feet give way as if someone greased the stairs while I was up there. Whap! I tumble down, and my butt smacks the floor. Since when did I become clumsy? I can dribble a soccer ball up and down the field and in and out of the orange cones without a problem. Hints of laughter grow into a loud crescendo, forcing Dam to rev up her clapping to quiet everyone.

Me and my red face slink back to my seat. A moment of success slides into humiliation in a split second as kids snicker when I pass.

Max slaps me on the shoulder as I plop into my seat and says, "Hope you enjoyed your trip, dude."

I'm about to tell him I didn't trip when I remember that silly suitcase and Ted jabbering on about me taking a trip. This is just like his yelling to me about the change in direction of the soccer ball. It's as if he knows what will happen before it does, or he has evil powers so he makes bad stuff happen, especially to me.

When he's involved, strange things happen. He isn't fooling me. But it's my duty as the son to unfool Mom.

CHAPTER 5

My butt is still sore when I get to my usual table in the cafeteria. Max gives me a thumbs-up but doesn't talk because his mouth is glued shut with Marshmallow Fluff. Once he swallows and takes a drink, he speaks. "Check out my double-decker fluffernutter."

He's lucky he no longer has to eat the slop they call chipped beef at Tucker Middle. Since Sammy's arrival, his mom has a major case of the guilts that Max isn't getting enough attention so she makes all his lunches and pampers him like he's a toddler.

"Can I see your certificate?" Madison asks. I hand her the envelope. She looks at it and passes it around, but I retrieve it just before Max gets his gooey fingers on it.

"There's another paper inside," Madison says and pulls it out. "It's some sort of scholarship to a program in New Hampshire."

I take the paper from her and read about the full scholarship to three weeks at the Lakeside Arts and Writing program.

"Nice, but I'm not going," I say.

"Why not, Rocket Boy?" Olive asks.

"Me and Max have soccer training camp this summer, and I have to be there if I want to make varsity in the ninth grade." High school is only four months away. Dad and I dreamed about me trying out for varsity in my first year, which is something few can achieve. Starting with peewee soccer, Dad had so many plans for my soccer career and insisted I had the goods to be a great goalie. Mom would get annoyed that he was overdoing the praise.

I remember when she once said to him, "Ron, really? He's only eight."

"I smell college scholarships in the air," Dad replied and tipped his nose up high and sniffed in as if he had to suck back a ton of snot. Sometimes he could be so funny.

After Olive reads the scholarship letter, she says, "Are you kidding? This is a huge deal. A kid two houses down from me went there a few years ago and had three Ivy League colleges fighting for him. That could be you."

"I'm going to a college with a ranked soccer team." Max and I high-five each other to cement that deal.

"Your choice," Madison says, dismissing the subject. "Now back to graduation. Are you wearing a skirt?" Madison asks. She is Tucker Middle's unofficial fashionista who always dresses for maximum attention with bright colors, mismatched socks, and tons of eye makeup.

Max chokes trying to empty his mouth quickly, because he's laughing so hard. Finally he speaks. "Madison, thanks for asking, but nix on the skirt for me unless you want us to go as twins."

"Big comedian," Olive says, and swings her body to face Madison and shut out Max and me from their convo.

The girls throw out a gazillion ideas for their outfits. They'll have to be wearing layers and layers of clothing to fit everything on.

The bell rings, and Olive and I set up an after-school meeting at our spot. We have to talk about Ted and the "other woman" in the photo. Also, I need her approval on my Plan B.

It's amazing how much has happened in the short time since Mom's big news.

AT THREE O'CLOCK I find Olive leaning against the wall, and we head over to the field for some privacy.

"The photo might have a simple explanation. You can't rush to judgment," Olive advises after I describe the woman and two kids with Ted. She sits on the grass and plays with the loose threads in the knee-holes of her jeans. I sit next to her.

"And I can't get Ted's criminal records without a credit card. I could go to the police station and ask them if they have him in their computers."

"Do not do that. Get real, Rocky. A kid walks in and asks a police officer if someone has a record. They'll want to know what he did to you, and they will for sure call your mother. And he didn't do anything to you."

"Maybe he did do something," I say and reach into my backpack for two chocolate-covered oat bars and give one to Olive.

"Like what?" She bites off a hunk of the bar.

"Ted claimed he'd never been to a soccer game before and then shouted instructions to me from the bleachers about how I should block a kick."

"So?"

"Um...his advice turned out to be right, but how does a guy who's never been to a game know anything about how to play? And later he gives me a suitcase, which is a terrible present and tells me I may take a trip, and today I trip down the stairs. Strange events."

Olive munches on the bar. "Coincidences, maybe, but put everything suspicious on your list. If these continue, you might be on to something. Speaking of having something, do you have any water?"

"No. Why do parents have to go and upset your life just when you seem to be gliding along as if someone oiled the bottoms of your shoes? It's not fair." I lean back on the grass and study the slow-moving clouds overhead.

"No one promises fair," Olive says and clutches her bent knees. "Tell me your Plan B."

"Ted lives in East Milton, and I refuse to move there and have to take the disgusting bus to high school. Even if I can't stop the wedding, I have to make sure I stay with Grandpa. I plan to make a case for him needing my help."

Olive says, "The bus! The odor on there is horrifying no matter how often they clean it, especially when kids get on right after P.E. But your mom would never agree to you not living with her. I could never live without my mom. I'd die if I had to move."

"My plan is foolproof. Mom will have no choice but to let me stay here," I continue. "If she says 'no,' it will be as if she's throwing Grandpa under the bus." I laugh at my pun. "She won't be able to say no."

"Good thinking. My skills are rubbing off on you." Olive smiles. "Maybe I will promote you to a junior plotter of plots. Got to go. Text later."

I walk home, grateful my guts aren't getting scrambled bouncing around on the nauseating bus. At least I have a Plan B in my back pocket.

By the time I'm at the back door, I'm in a celebration mood, thinking Mom might take me for ice cream after dinner. She'll want to frame the certificate for sure.

I reach into my jeans pocket for the key before I remember there's a new programmable lock. Mom allowed Ted to install it. It's Grandpa's house, and he should have objected, but he didn't. Come to think of it, Ted has a way of involving himself in a lot of things around here, and they let him.

After Ted set up the lock, he assumed it was his job to drill the code into me. He made me repeat it a gazillion times, as if my memory is like a strainer trying to hold water. What an insult to a kid who'll be fourteen in a few months.

The door opens, and it is kinda cool not to have to use a key, but I'm not telling Ted that.

I dump my backpack and shoes and head into the den to say hi to Grandpa. He's in his plushy lounge chair with the foot part raised. That man loves his books almost as much as he loves me and Mom. Sitting and reading has become even more important considering his hip is giving him lots of grief, and he doesn't walk unless he has to.

"Grandpa, do you need anything?" I ask, already rehearsing for my audition as his chief helper.

"I'm fine. Go get something to eat."

I open cabinets and the refrigerator multiple times on my snack hunt. When nothing speaks to me, I give up and take out the chocolate Cheerios, the most reliable go-to food.

When I finish eating, I head upstairs and although I should do biology first, I snap up my writing notebook and green pen, the color for inspiration. There's an idea flying around my brain for a new story I want to get on paper before I forget it. After I write about three paragraphs, I stop and reread the scene. This writing is way different from my usual stories. It's a sci-fi about implanted chips that parents use to get complete access to everything their kid does. I like it. Will def have to show this to Ms. Rotterdam at my next creative writing class and get her take on whether writing about a giant talking bird is lame.

I turn to biology homework. By the time Mom's car pulls into the driveway around six o'clock, I have finished my homework and hustle downstairs with my award envelopes in hand.

Mom is already working on dinner and still sporting her ginormous grin, accompanied by sunbeams popping out of her face. Her clients must have been baffled all day that their sane accountant has gone fruit loops. Even Mom describes most accountants, except for her, as dull. I expect her smile to get even bigger, if that's possible, once I share my good news.

I'm glad Ted isn't here tonight, and it's only the three of us like before he glued himself to my family.

Once we start to eat, I say, "Nice to have dinner, just us." Mom has to know the truth, my truth. "Because I have some news."

I pass Mom the large envelope with the award certificate. She takes it out and studies it for a sec, before leaping up to wrap me in a tight hug.

"Rocky, this is fantastic! You are so talented. Congratulations. Pop, you've got to see this." She hands Grandpa the certificate.

While he's reading, she removes the second paper, which describes the Lakeside program. Then she exclaims, "Wowie! Wow! A full scholarship to the Lakeside Arts and Writing program. Amazing."

I twirl some pasta on my fork and bask in the glory that is mine.

"Three whole weeks in the mountains of New Hampshire," she says.

"But I'm not going."

"Why not?" Mom asks.

"Duh. Soccer camp. Remember? They've got a pro goalie coming special to train me. Coach Taylor thinks I might make varsity in the ninth grade. Dad would've been stoked."

Grandpa puts down the certificate. "Way to go. My grandson, the author."

Mom says, "Soccer is important, but you should recognize you have other talents too."

When we're almost done with dinner, the back door squeaks open, and shoes thud against the kitchen floor. This has to be Ted because, besides us, he's the only one who has a code to the lock. It's as if he owns the place. Ted walks into the dining room and puts a brown bag on the table.

"Ice cream," he says, unpacking the bag. Why did he bring ice cream tonight? There's no way he could've known about the award in advance because I only just told Mom a few minutes ago. I doubt that Dam clued her in ahead of time. Teachers usually don't do that.

"There's mint chocolate chip for you, Rocky. You seem like a mint chip sort of guy," Ted says.

Mom must've divulged all my personal info to Ted. I consider that borderline traitorous. Mom brings out bowls and spoons, and he scoops out some mint chip and hands it to me.

No way am I giving Ted a victory, so I pass it back to him and say, "I prefer coffee flavor."

"Oh, I thought..." I watch with satisfaction as his smile goes poof. "Sorry, Rocky," he says. His face now resembles someone whose dog just ran away. He was ready to make a big splash with the mint chip, and it was an epic fail.

"Okay, I'll take vanilla," I say.

"Sorry, no vanilla either."

Mom shoots me the stink eye. She's on to my game, so I drop the sparring match and say, "I guess it will have to be mint chip."

After drowning my ice cream in hot fudge sauce, Mom tells Ted about my award.

"Congratulations, buddy," he says.

When he calls me "buddy," my mouth goes all pukey even though I'm eating ice cream.

He continues, "The Lakeside writing program has an outstanding reputation."

I put down my spoon and lick off some misguided fudge from under my bottom lip. "I'm not going. I signed up for soccer camp this summer. You know, I might be a famous goalie someday and make a fortune because of this training camp." Okay, that's a huge exaggeration, but still …

Ted says, "Lakeside is a superb program, not to be missed. I have a hunch you'll change your mind and pass on soccer camp this summer."

"Your hunch is wrong," I say in my brattiest voice. "I have more homework to do," which I do not, but it always works as a ticket to disappear. I scoop up my award papers and leave.

Why does Ted even get to have hunches about my life?

CHAPTER 6

A day later, while we're waiting for the after-school bus to drive the team to an away soccer game, Max unloads a joke bomb complete with fart sound effects. Even Marco groans. Max's idea of funny hasn't advanced out of sixth grade, even though most of the guys have moved on from gross boy humor. I'm relieved when the bus arrives.

At the field, we do our usual warmup routines until Coach Taylor calls us together for a pregame meeting to present the lowdown on the Quincy Badgers.

He says, "The Badgers are formidable." It's typical of Coach to try to scare us into staying sharp, but this time he has additional incentive to charge us up. "Win this game, and you're in the regionals and may make all-state for middle school."

I run on to the field and situate myself in front of the net. Within the first five minutes, I allow one goal and only because they had a penalty shot, which is almost impossible to block. It is so not my fault. The game proceeds without letup and a hundred shots come at me, but I manage to block them all.

Tan and Marco dribble as if they're one body after stealing the ball from a Badger, and Tan evens the score. The other team continues to bear down on me, and I dive to my left for a block. My cleats catch a large divot, and I hit the ground with a thud, grabbing my foot as a scream emerges that I can't squelch. I saved the goal, but instead of leaping up in victory, I struggle to stand and hop around like a gigantic, one-legged kangaroo before I fall back down. Coach Taylor runs on to the field.

"Are you okay?" Coach asks, examining the chunk of grass I dislodged.

"Foot," I answer.

"Can you walk?"

"Dunno." I try to get up again, but the pain soars up my leg and brings tears to my eyes. I squeeze them back, using the technique I perfected after Dad died when people were always around and I was determined to keep my tears as private property, not to be shared with anyone.

The other team's coach comes over and says, "Is he okay? This is awful. A fluke. These fields are always perfect. They're the pride of Quincy. The town poured millions into rehabbing this area."

Coach Taylor nods his head. "They're almost as nice as our Skyline Field. Nothing shabby here. Help me get this kid into my car."

The two coaches lock hands together to make a seat, and I scramble on. They carry me off the field, depositing me into Coach Taylor's car while he calls for an ambulance. All the guys gather around to wave and promise they'll bury the Badgers for me. *Yeah, you wish.* The defense better step up their game if the Tigers have a prayer of winning this one.

The ambulance arrives without a siren. I'm not an emergency. The guys put me on a bed inside, and Coach Taylor gets in with me.

I ask, "Where are they taking me?"

"ER," Coach answers and commands Siri to call Marybeth Casson.

"Ms. Casson, I mean Marybeth, this is Coach Taylor. Rocky took a little spill at the game."

Pause.

"His foot," Coach says.

Pause.

"Quincy Hospital Emergency off Blue Hill Avenue."

Pause.

"Twenty minutes or shorter if they put the siren on."

The ambulance dude shakes his head, "No siren."

Coach stretches his arm out to bring the phone closer to me and says, "Rocky, shout 'hello' to your mom so she knows you're okay."

I suck it up and try to speak normally through the pain. "Mom. I'm. Okay."

"Don't worry, Marybeth, he'll be fine. See you soon."

At the hospital, the guys wheel me in, and Coach follows. He talks to someone at a desk, and a man in a hospital uniform takes over, pushing me down a corridor to an X-ray room. The nurse helps me onto a white, cold table and jostles my foot as she props it on a pillow for the X-rays. It hurts like heck to be in that position.

When they're finished, two people plunk me back into the wheelchair and roll me into another room. Mom and Coach are there waiting for me. Mom pushes the hair off my forehead and plants a kiss there. "It must be so painful." Her eyes are wet. She'd better not cry over an injured foot. This isn't life or death like when we rushed from the airport to the hospital to see Dad. And got there too late.

A doctor comes in and fiddles with the computer until the pictures of my foot are on his screen. There are so many pieces of bone. It's fascinating how all those pieces fit together. Amazing engineering.

The doctor touches my foot all over, and I tighten my lips to keep the howls from getting out. That foot is already swollen to twice the size of the other one.

"There are many bones in the foot," the doctor explains. "Twenty-six to be exact. So many possibilities for breaks. Your son broke two metatarsals. The good news is the bones are not dislocated, and no surgery is required."

Mom pats my hand and fills the room with her exaggerated sigh.

The doctor continues, "The bad news is no soccer for at least six weeks."

"That's not possible," I say, "Soccer camp starts in a month."

"No soccer," the doctor repeats, and shoots me an eye arrow to indicate this isn't up for discussion.

The doctor writes on a notepad in front of him and doesn't look up while he says, "He'll wear a boot so he can put some weight on it and get around without crutches. I treat too many incidents of kids coming in with another injury from a crutches mishap."

"So, he'll be fine?" Mom asks.

"Absolutely." The doctor assures her. "Hairline fractures, no displacement. He'll be back on the field before you know it."

"Thank you," she says, smiling, not caring how devastating this is for me. *Mom, I have plans, a career to think about.*

"Down the hall. Room C. They'll fit him for a boot, which he'll wear for four weeks. When you finish there, make a follow-up appointment."

An hour or so later, the boot is on, Coach Taylor leaves, and Mom parks my wheelchair near the door and heads out to bring her car around. While I sit and wait, I review the soccer play responsible for my fate. My cleats got stuck, which happens only once in a — or maybe never. No one I know has caught a divot like that before. Too many bad things happening to me lately. Can't be a coincidence.

When we pull into the driveway, Mom texts, and in a flash, Ted bounds out of the house and opens the car door.

"Are you okay?" he asks as his eyebrows dance. "Must be painful. Put your arm around my shoulder." It's cringey to have to touch him, but I have no choice. Grandpa's not strong enough to help me. Ted lifts me out and practically carries me inside, placing me on the sofa as if I'm as delicate as Max's baby. Ted's stronger than he looks for such a skinny guy.

Ted says, "I know you're disappointed about no soccer camp this summer, but you're lucky to have such an outstanding alternative program. Remember, I had a hunch you would go to Lakeside, and now you will. Everything works out as it should."

I think I detect him gloating as if this was a contest between him and me, and I lost.

And he has the you-know-whats to call this lucky.

CHAPTER 7

The effects of the pill they gave me in the ER are wearing off, so even a tiny movement sends piercing bursts of pain up my leg. Mom brings in blankets, sheets and pillows, so I guess I'm sleeping down here tonight.

She plumps up a pillow and places it under my foot, explaining, "Elevating it will keep the swelling down. No stairs until tomorrow. If you need something from your room, just ask."

Grandpa pats me on the head and says, "You'll be back in top shape soon."

I spy Ted lurking in the doorway, surveying the scene. Then he speaks. "Take a day off tomorrow. Watch videos or do that Xbox thing you always talk about. I can work from here and hang with you."

Mom flashes him her over-gleeful smile as she pulls up a chair next to me. "That's so nice of you, Ted. I have an important meeting, but I'll do my best to get home early." She turns her face toward me, and I see sadness in her eyes. "Rocky, I'm so sorry this happened to you for two reasons."

Okay, so now she does understand this accident came at the worst possible time and is tragic. But what is her second reason?

"Two?" I ask.

"First, I hate when you're hurt and in pain." This sends a tiny tear trickling down her cheek, which she swipes away. She must've freaked when she got the call from Coach Taylor in the middle of the afternoon.

"It's not so bad now," I say, because it's not my thing to give her extra worry. I continue, "The boot does an excellent job of holding all those little bones in place. But soccer camp is not happening, and I could lose my chance to perfect my goalie moves before high school. Dad and I—"

Mom interrupts, "You and your dad made lots of grand plans for your soccer future, and you will be a star at Milton High. The doctor promised you'll be fine when you're healed, if you follow instructions. How proud Dad would be knowing you've become an award-winning writer too." She pushes the bangs out of my eyes.

Would he? I'm not so sure. I never did creative writing before Dam's English class this year. Soccer is what still connects Dad and me.

"What's your other reason?" I ask.

"Now, you'll go to Lakeside for three entire weeks, and I'll miss you terribly."

Ted walks over carrying a mug and a plate of cookies. He's so stealthy. One minute he's here, and then he's gone without a sound to alert you. That's spooky.

He sets the tray down on a table next to me. "These are special dunking cookies for your hot chocolate. They're filled with caramel, which melts in the warm liquid."

I dunk as instructed and take a bite. The caramel is creamy, and the cookie is awesome. Got to give him props for this snack.

"Really good," I say.

Ted replies, "Glad you like it. The hot chocolate and the cookie are a team, like rice and beans, PB and J, hot dogs and mustard... They have to be together."

Why is this guy suddenly reciting dopey food pairs? Mom is so gaga to get married she either doesn't notice or doesn't care about the durky things he says. I'm adding this weirdness to my list of reasons why she shouldn't marry him.

"Can I get some water?" I say.

Ted replies, "I'm on it."

And he's off as if his life depends on this mission. He returns in no time. He's like a servant responding to my command. I wonder if that's a sign he feels guilty about my broken foot because I'm sure it's his fault I'm in this situation.

⸙

When I wake the next morning, I check my phone through half-cracked eyelids, amazed that I slept until eleven. The day can really zoom by when you're not in school in countdown mode until three o'clock.

On my way to pee, I spot Ted and Grandpa at the kitchen table. My heavy boot doesn't let me slip by unheard.

"Hey, guy," Ted calls out. "How you doing this beautiful morning?" Mom must have warned him off the use of *buddy*, so now I'm *guy*. Whatever.

"Okay," I reply and keep walking.

"Order anything you want for breakfast. Your wish will be done," Ted stands and bows as if before a king and chuckles. I close the bathroom door.

When I open it, I almost bonk Ted in the nose because he's stationed himself right outside.

"So?" he says.

"Um...cereal is fine. I can get it myself."

"For today, I'm here to wait on you. Go into the den, and I'll bring it to you."

He comes in with a bowl of cereal sloshing around in lots of milk, just the way I like it. I suspect Mom has been tutoring him on all things Rocky. She's working overtime on getting me to like him, but it isn't fair because she isn't also schooling me on Ted and his crazy ways. so I'm at a disadvantage here. But I'm too famished now to dwell on him. I eat as if I've been on a long fast.

After Ted clears the bowl, he asks, "So what do you want to do? Play a game? Monopoly?"

"I'm going to play FIFA. It's a video soccer game."

"I'll play with you."

"Did you ever play FIFA on the Xbox?" I ask him.

"No, but I'm sure it's fun."

This bozo is so arrogant. He thinks playing FIFA is simple, that he can do it with no instruction and no experience. I set up the game and give him a controller. He holds it upside down, but I don't correct him. He's not asking for help, so I offer none. When I finish with him, he'll be in FIFA disgrace.

By the time Ted gets the controller figured out, I'm already leading 2-0. This will be a piece of cake.

Ted says, "Thank you for introducing me to a new game." A minute later, he says, "I just scored a point!" and raises his hand for a high five, but I pretend I don't see it. "I'm catching on. It's exciting."

"I guess," I mumble.

"The players' faces are so realistic. The miracles of hi-tech are a marvel, don't you agree?"

"Yeah." I wish he'd shut up. He's messing with my concentration to throw me off my game. The next time he speaks, I'm gonna tell him talking isn't allowed during the game.

But he shuts his trap and scores point after point in rapid succession. I use my T-shirt to dry sweat beads off my nonexistent mustache. The game ends, and my thumbs are numb. Ted wiped the floor with me. The final score is 11-2. This is the worst game of my life. Me, a champion player, losing to an amateur. Impossible. No way he could pull that off unless he's been lying about playing this before.

"How did you do that?" I ask.

"Do what?" Pretending to be innocent is the biggest fake out. Everyone knows that trick. Not too subtle, Ted.

"How did you win?" He should know he's under suspicion.

"Just did. So much fun. We can have a rematch later."

"How many times have you played before? Be honest." I push back.

"I never played a video game on the Xbox before. This was my first time. I didn't even know how to hold the controller, but I got the hang of it. I did okay after that."

"Yeah."

I lift my heavy booted foot and start to hike up the stairs to the shower.

Ted rushes over to try to assist me and puts an arm around me as if he's about to pick me up.

"Put me down! Mom said I could do the stairs today if I go slow."

"I can help you."

"I think you have helped enough."

He calls after me, "We can play another game after lunch."

No more games until I figure out what this trickster is up to.

CHAPTER 8

Two days later, Mom has taken me off the injured list and okayed my return to school. Couldn't come soon enough. I'm about to lose my mind with Ted's hovering, which I'm sure is a clear sign of his guilty conscience.

Mom insists on driving me, claiming the walk is too far, but I think she needs more time to pile on the do's and don'ts. If she's so worried about me, she should talk to Ted about my recent accidents. I have no proof, but too many bad things keep happening to me since he's in the picture.

I open the car door, and Mom adds, "And remember go slow on the stairs. No racing. If your foot gets painful, check in with the nurse immediately."

"Enough already. I will."

At school, the boot brings me some attention, but the main buzz today is on the first rehearsal for the eighth-grade graduation. Because the teachers don't want me standing too long, I'm assigned the role of an important person who sits on the stage and shakes hands with each kid as they get their diploma.

By the time we're done, I'd sell my favorite soccer ball for a gallon of Purell to clean off all the germs from the snotty, sweaty paws that touched me, but I'll have to settle for soap in the restroom.

After I've cleaned up, I go to Ms. Rotterdam's class and stand by her desk waiting for her to notice me so I can ask if she'll read my new story. I'm worried about the opening. I know she cares about that a ton, because she pounds it into us that the beginning has to capture the reader's attention and hook them into turning the pages.

"Leave it with me," she replies, displaying two rows of teeth too-perfect for an old person. They might be fakes. "I'll write some edit notes for you. You can pick up your notebook in class tomorrow."

She lowers her glasses so they hang on her chest, which serves as a kind of shelf for them. She has the most outstanding collection of shirts in the world, and the one she's wearing today is rad. Printed across the front, it says: *Careful, or you'll end up in my novel.* Hilarious. Got to give her kudos for an excellent sense of humor.

Dam puts my notebook in her large cloth bag and says, "Sorry about your foot, but I understand your injury seals the deal for you to go to Lakeside. This is a fantastic opportunity. Althea Williams will teach there this summer. I hope you can get in her workshop. She's an extraordinary talent and a beautiful human being. She'll show you how to write characters that will leap off the page and are authentic and layered."

"Okay," I reply, unenthusiastic about a summer without soccer.

"Also, you have an excellent shot at winning the national prize if you work hard there. The winner gets a free trip to the awards ceremony in Los Angeles."

Holy moly! Los Angeles! Now she's got my attention. That's the home of the training headquarters for the United States men's soccer team. Dad and I dreamed we'd go there someday. That memory causes a sadness to bubble up inside me, but I clamp it down before it boils over. Dad would be pumped if I won that trip, which is all the incentive I need to write one heck of a story.

"I'll do better than my best," I promise her.

She smiles, assuming I'm excited to dive into my creative writing, but soccer is still number one for me like it was for Dad.

When English class ends, I snail-walk along the hallway toward the cafeteria. I take an end seat at our table so I can stretch out my bad leg.

Still in graduation mode, Olive says, "We need our own special graduation celebration."

"I don't even want to go to the ceremony," I say.

"Why not?" Max asks.

"Because Ted will be there with my mom in front of everyone like it's normal."

"Well, it isn't abnormal. You just don't like it," Olive says. "Okay, I'll help you, as usual, even if I don't agree with you. Tell your mom you can only get two tickets for her and your grandpa."

This little lie might work if Mom doesn't check in with the school office. They said you could ask for extra tickets, but this is worth a try for sure.

"Awesome. Thanks, I'll do that," I reply.

"Let's go to Regina's Pizza Saturday night," Olive says.

"Wow, it's like a dat—" Max stops midsentence, before he utters the *date* word.

"Excellent," I say.

Madison winks at Max, and his cheeks get all pink, as if he just got caught in the cafeteria with Marshmallow Fluff up his nose. I have a lot of work to do to get him ready for this dat—I mean, pizza party.

"What else is going on with *him*?" Olive asks.

"Him who?" Max chimes in.

"Ted."

Max goes back to stuffing his face because his mom always packs a ton of food, and his mouth doesn't quit chomping until the bell rings.

"I suspect he's responsible somehow for my broken foot," I say, knowing how whacky that sounds.

Max's mouth twists into awkward angles as he tries to swallow so much sticky Fluff and PB. On another day, I'd be in hysterics watching him. He frees his mouth and says, "You're loco, bro. How could he do that? He wasn't even at the game."

"I don't know how he did it, but he did."

Olive says, "Rocket Man, perhaps your mind is too soaked in fiction, and you dream up unrealistic situations that don't happen in real life." She swings her ponytail in a swoony way, trying to lighten my mood, but this is darn serious.

She continues, "Speaking of writing. I have an idea for your next story. Write about Ted and all his craziness. Then your mom can read it and know the truth about him. She'll be forced to call off the wedding."

"I could do that. I'm working on a bird story now, but I could write an exposé of Ted when I'm at Lakeside." And in a flash, this plan takes shape. I'll demolish Ted in my story and win the trip to L.A. This will be the best twofer ever. A speck of hope loosens up my tight muscles.

On our way out of the cafeteria, I pretend-sock Max in the gut and say, "Call me about Saturday. It's gonna be fun, but there are rules."

"Like what?" His eyebrows climb up his forehead, producing a confused, dumb expression.

"Later, man."

On my way down the hall on the second floor to Spanish, I

freeze at the sight of Mom and Ted walking into Ms. Rotterdam's office.

They never even told me they were meeting with her.

CHAPTER 3

I swivel 180 degrees and take the east staircase to the first-floor, shuffle along the corridor as fast as the boot allows, and then clump up the west staircase back to the second floor. What a long route. Why wouldn't Mom tell me she has an appointment with Rotterdam? And why did she drag *him* with her? A muddle of questions clogs my brain pipes.

Of course, my maneuvers make me late for class, but a broken foot should buy me some forgiveness today. I stare at the clock above the teacher's desk and try to telepathically urge the little hand to go faster.

When the last bell rings, I head out to meet Grandpa, who's picking me up today on Mom's orders.

"How did you get around?" he asks, as I settle into the car.

"No problem. Grandpa. Can I ask you a question?"

"Sure," he says, pulling away from school.

"Isn't Ted strange sometimes? He beat me at FIFA the other day, even though supposedly it was his first time playing. How's that possible?"

"I guess he's a quick study and wicked smart. He must've copied what you were doing. You can call it beginner's luck. There's always a spot of truth in those old clichés."

"Maybe."

As he parks the car, Grandpa says, "Ted makes your mom happy, and that's important. He's trying his best with you. You've got to give it time."

"Give it time" is another ridiculous thing adults pull out of their stash when they don't have a good reason for something. I had a belly full of ridiculous expressions flung at me after Dad died, like "You'll be the man of the house from now on" or, the one I hate the most, "He's in a better place." Dad's better place is here practicing soccer with me.

Inside the house, I skip my usual snack, because I have to tell Olive ASAP about Mom's mysterious meeting.

She picks up the call fast. "What's wrong? I can smell trouble through the phone."

"Mom and Ted were in school today talking to Dam."

"About what?"

"I have no idea."

"Didn't you ask them?"

"No, I avoided them."

Olive says, "You should've strolled over and said all casual-like, 'I didn't know you two go to Tucker,' and then after everyone laughs, you could ask why they're there."

"I was too shocked to do anything."

"Maybe they wanted to thank Dam for giving you the big award." Olive spins their visit in a positive way, but it doesn't compute. Mom would've told me that.

"Technically, Dam didn't give it to me. She submitted my story to a contest."

"Whatev. So, they wanted to thank her for submitting your story. You're getting all worked up. Ask your mom, and call me when you find out."

"Okay. Gotta go. Max is texting."

Max: Rules for Saturday? He sends an emoji with a stupid grinning face.

Me: No hugging or holding hands or anything unless you ask consent, and a girl's 100% okay with it.

Max: I know that.

Me: AND NO FART JOKES.

I add a face-plant emoji to that text.

Max: Do I have to pay for her pizza? I'm not sure my dad will give me enough money.

Me: You don't pay for her, and she doesn't pay for you. That way, she doesn't owe you, and you don't owe her. And don't be your usual dingbat self. Be cool.

Max: I'm psyched. GTG.

Max isn't the smoothest guy at Tucker, so it's kinda up to me to prevent him from making an ox of himself.

A little after six o'clock, I clunk down the stairs in my noisy boot. Ted's putting two large brown bags on the counter and says, "Bought Chinese."

Mom sets out plates, chopsticks, and napkins on the kitchen island and says, "Buffet. Serve yourself."

Grandpa takes some of everything. I pile my plate with lo mein, scallion pancakes, and Peking ravioli.

I glance at Mom, and once again she's competing for the *Guinness Book of Records* for massive monster smiles. Her eyes are on a continuous loop from me to Ted as if she's bursting to say something. OMG. I pray no more announcements. The blood in my veins goes icy. I shudder.

"Are you okay, Rocky?" Mom asks.

I'm scared to ask about their visit to Rotterdam because I'm pretty sure I won't like the answer, so instead I say, "I can only get two tickets for graduation."

Mom doesn't skip a beat and says, "No problem. Grandpa won't be going anyway. He can't sit for that long in a hard chair. It'll be Ted and me cheering you on."

Nothing seems to cut my way. Ted will be at graduation.

"Me and Olive and a couple of other kids want to celebrate our graduation at Regina's pizza tomorrow night. Will you give me a ride?"

"Sure," Mom says.

"Can we pick up Max?"

"Of course," she replies, as Ted offers her a wonton, and she lets him pop it into her mouth. Ick to the tenth power.

"Regina's. Hmmm," Ted mutters.

"What does hmmm mean?" I ask.

"Pino's is the best pizza place in Milton," he says.

"Well, Regina's my favorite," I say. He's such a control freak, trying to take over the decision where I will go for pizza. He must think I have a chip imbedded in me that he can switch on and force me to do whatever he wants. Think again, Bozo, there's no link between us.

"Pino's is better," the big know-it-all insists. So now he's an expert on pizza and soccer.

"We're going to Regina's for sure," I say, ending that discussion. "A kid told me you were both at Tucker today." I don't mention that kid was me.

"Yes, we were," Ted says cheerfully, as if there's nothing better than a day at a middle school.

"Why were you there?"

I'm surprised Mom lets Ted step in to answer first. "We spoke to Ms. Rotterdam about Lakeside and spaghetti and meatballs. Get it? Bacon and eggs..."

"Spaghetti and meatballs?" I repeat, confused by another of Ted's crazy comments.

"Things that belong together," he explains.

Mom jumps in to join in this dumb game and adds, "Mac 'n cheese."

Ted laughs. I'm happy they're enjoying their recitation of food pairs. Ted continues, "Or like Hansel and Gretel, Shrek and Donkey, Batman and Robin—some pairs always have to be together."

Mom's head snaps back in husky laughter.

"Like you and your mom shouldn't be apart," he adds. "So, we're coming with you to Lakeside!"

CHAPTER 10

My ears must've disconnected from my brain. What I just heard is impossible, unbelievable, outrageous, and UNFAIR.

I suck in a lungful of air to restart my breathing. The shriek that exits from my mouth is a cross between a squeak and a shout that makes my head vibrate. "Mom, how could you do this to me?"

Her lips pull into a straight line as she loses the smile. "Ted thought—"

"Ted doesn't get a say here," I interrupt.

But that doesn't stop him from butting in. "I only want your mom to be happy. She told me how anxious she'll be with you away from home for three whole weeks."

So now he's guilting me that I'm the one who's preventing Mom from being happy. Hey, buddy, I was making her happy long before she knew you. He makes me seem like the big, fat, smelly turd in all this. How did my life get so twisted? If she marries him, I'm staying with Grandpa for sure, and that will not be negotiable.

"This will be like a pre-honeymoon for all of us," Mom says. The word "honeymoon" steams me. Why is everything always about the wedding? She continues, "Ted had this marvelous idea. I will volunteer to assist their accountant, and he will work on the construction of their new social hall."

Ted. Ted. Ted. I've got to get rid of him. He has no clue about the delicate dance between teenagers and parents, and how they're supposed to stay out of a kid's life. Ted keeps stepping on my already broken metatarsals.

"Rocky, I'll get to see you every day." Mom sings her words, as if she's performing a top ten hit. "That means so much to me."

I add a heaping helping of firmness to my voice and say, "No thirteen-year-old wants their mother at overnight camp. Absolutely no one!"

"Hey, you guys belong together like pancakes and syrup." Ted tries to chuckle his way out of this mess he created.

"Trust me, it will be great," Mom says.

Trust you. You're allowing Ted to take over our lives. My only way out of this is to tell her if they're are at Lakeside, I'm not going. But then I'll have no soccer camp and no chance to win a trip to Los Angeles either. *Dad,* I call inside my head, *What should I do?*

No answer. That's the problem when your dad dies: he's not there when you need him, and I need him badly. Then again, if he were here, there'd be no Ted in my life. The only upside to this fiasco is if they're at Lakeside, they can't run off and get married. It buys me time.

"If I agree to this," I say, "you must promise to keep a low—and I mean lower than a coal mine shaft—profile. Just pretend you never met me."

Mom locks her crystal blue eyes on mine. "Of course, Rocky. We won't even talk to you when we pass in the dining hall, I promise."

Ted smiles as if he received the citizen-of-the-year award. He set this up from the moment I broke my foot. Heck, I bet he loosened the turf in front of the goal just to arrange all this. He is the devil, and not only because of that dark patch of hair residing on his chin.

"Homework," I say to get out of there right away and talk to Olive.

I text her.

Me: I found out why they were at Tucker.

Olive: ?????

Me: They're going with me.

Olive: Cryptic, Rocket Man. Where are they going?

Me: Lakeside

Olive: You're kidding!!!!!! Call me.

I stop texting and phone her. "Mom and Ted plan to work at Lakeside while I'm there so they, I mean Mom, won't have to miss me. That's why they were meeting with Dam. They'll be up in my business all summer."

"So, are you afraid they'll cramp your style?"

"What style?" I say. "I have a ton of work to do there writing a blockbuster story, starring the villain known as Ted."

"And they'll both be there when you read it and annihilate him. Perfect. As a bonus, you can't be blamed for your excellent fiction writing. Ha. Ha."

"My mighty green pen, in all its glory, will end this wedding business, and Mom can't get mad at me for writing a great story. You're a genius."

"I know, and you're lucky I'm geniusing on your behalf," Olive says.

"I'm gonna start working on it tonight. I'll have to figure out a way to add something about how Ted tampered with the sod near the goal."

"Whoa, Rockala. Lose your mind much? How could he do that? Perhaps you got a concussion when you fell."

"My head never touched the ground. He said something

suspicious before the game. I'll explain tomorrow. I want you to know everything in case..." I hesitate.

"In case what?" she asks.

"In case anything worse than a couple of broken foot bones happens to me."

🗎

BEFORE I GO TO BED, I start my story and name the main character DET so Ted can't sue me. *Now, green pen, is the time for you to do your magic.*

The High Councilor sits on his throne, which rises from the floor so he is higher than the rest of us. His long beard curls up in his lap like a gray kitten, and he even pats it from time to time. He wears a golden robe ~~on~~ which drapes around his mountain of a stomach that is held together with a purple sash. Only the top person is allowed to wear those colors. He looks like a throwback to old-time fantasy figures that I've seen in my history tablet, people like Santa Claus and Dumbledore.

The High Councilor commands everyone's attention with a wave of his electronic wand that shoots a lightning bolt from one end of the room to the other, as he calls the meeting of The Council of Martian Undercover Operations to order. His voice is so loud some people cover their ears when he talks.

He says, "This mission is designed to learn how to control Earth families, and it's crucial to Mars' goal of commanding other peoples ~~and being superiority~~ in the galaxy. I have appointed DET to be the first undercover operator to ruin an Earth family. I have ~~picked~~ chosen a simple assignment for this trial of a mother and her son. With no father present in the family, getting close to them should be as easy as doing somersaults in zero gravity. DET, do you have questions?"

DET stands and as he prepares to answer, his eyes change from steaming black tar to harsh yellow. That's the signal he is gathering up all his evil powers into one central spot in his brain. "I'm ready," DET says, brimming with confidence, "Can't wait to get there. I have planned a series of calamities for the boy before I take over his mother and his house."

The High Councilor lowers his chair, stands, and salutes DET. "Excellent. When you have destroyed that family, bring them here for a debriefing."

I shake out the kinks in my writing hand to restart the blood flow. Enough for now, my creative steam has evaporated. This story is even more brutal than what I planned. Mom will hate it, but I have no choice.

CHAPTER 11

I'm psyched for the pizza party when Saturday arrives. It's a dark, heavy rain day, and Mom has to detour because of a roadblock, so she drops Max and me off a block away from Regina's Pizza.

"Remember not to run in that boot. Do you want an umbrella?" Mom asks.

"Nah."

Poor Max has to slow-walk with me, and we arrive a bit wet. Olive and Madison are waiting outside the restaurant with open umbrellas. I can't understand why they didn't go inside to keep dry.

Madison winks at Max as usual.

"It's closed," Olive says.

"Huh?" Max says. "I'm starved."

"When aren't you starved?" I ask.

"We were counting on this party," Madison says, displaying her pink-glazed lips for Max. I bet she and Olive spent hours working on clothes and hair. Me, a dab of gel, and I'm ready to party.

"Guys," I say, "there's another pizza place called Pino's."

Now I'm thinking that Ted planted the idea of going to Pino's in my mind on purpose. Did he know Regina's would be closed, or did he use his powers to close Regina's? My suspicion factory is now working round-the-clock where Ted is concerned.

"Never heard of it, but let's go there," Madison says and turns to Max. "Come under my umbrella."

Max freezes with no idea what his next move should be. I walk over and stick my head under Olive's umbrella and take the handle from her to demonstrate. Max copies me, joining Madison under hers.

I type Pino's into my phone's GPS. It's only three blocks from here, and thanks to the girls' umbrellas, Max and I won't have to sit there in soggy clothes.

When I'm inside, I'm struck by the flashing neon signs lining the walls which are an assault on the eyes. A green one shouts *Buy by the slice!* and a red one offers a special price for an all-white pizza, which shouldn't even be allowed to exist, because authentic pizza must have red sauce.

At the counter, the girls order a slice of plain pizza each and diet drinks. I get two slices loaded with pepperoni and a large blue drink, which has a boatload of sugar, but there's no one here to tell me how bad that is for you, so what the heck. Tonight is special. Max watches my every move and orders the same.

In the booth, I sit beside Olive, and Madison scoots in on the other side. Max remains standing as if he never sat on a bench in his life. I nod at him and then at Madison, and he gets my message and eases himself down next to her.

Pino's slices are enormous, oily and super delicious, but eating them in front of girls might be tricky. I keep a pile of napkins ready for a mop-up job and glance at Max, hoping he doesn't totally embarrass himself with gobs of sauce running down his chin.

Olive says, "So dish about the man who's almost like your father-light. Get it? Like diet soda instead of real soda!"

"Hilarious. He will not be my father-light because I'm not letting my mom marry him." I put down the crust of the pizza so I won't be distracted into taking a bite while I give them the lowdown. I say, "Hear me out. You might think I just arrived from outer space or I'm allowing my imagination to run amok, but there's been some weird sh—"

I can't get out another sound even though my mouth opens and closes a few times. I must look like a fish flopping around on dry land, gasping for air. My body is in shock, as if I stuck a wet finger in the electric socket.

"Weird what?" Max asks.

Madison stares at me and rises from the bench as if she's gonna jump over the table and give me life support.

Max says, "Hey, man, you're freaking me out. What gives?"

At last, I'm able to emit the tiniest of whispers. "Turn around."

Max moves his entire mammoth body and then looks back at me with eyes that blink "danger" like a flashing red-light alarm in a diving submarine.

"Bam!" Max says.

I watch Ted head this way, oblivious that crashing a kids' party is a major sin. Even though he doesn't have kids, I'm shocked he doesn't know this rule, which has existed for since forever.

"Hi there, Rocky and friends," he says with his eyebrows doing their hop. "I thought you'd be at Regina's tonight. I guess you listened to me after all and decided to go for the best pizza in Milton. You won't be sorry."

"So nice to see you." Olive's voice is coated with honey. "Did you forget to tell Rocky about Regina's being closed?" She oozes sarcasm.

He says, "It's closed? Who knew?" His smug smile is a dead

giveaway. He planned this whole episode. "I'm just here to pick up pizza for Rocky's mom and me."

"What a coincidence." Olive's snarky tone breaks through, and I sense she's suspicious too.

"It certainly is." Ted replies. "I told Rocky Pino's is the best pizza in the world, but he insisted on Regina's."

"It is good," Max confirms, as he clamps down on the last bit of his last slice. I don't think he fully grasps how awful this is for me. With him, you have to spell out all the deets.

Ted says, "I'll wait here and drive you all home. The rain is coming down hard."

"That's so nice of you, but my mom is planning to pick us up," Olive says, and I applaud her quick save, so we don't have to ride with Ted.

Ted persists, "Call her and tell her she doesn't have to come. I'm already here."

He plunks himself down in the booth behind us. "You all take your time. Let me know when you're ready to go."

Now all I want is to get out of here immediately. Can't stand to stay another minute with him hovering there. The others sense my tension, because within a minute, all three of them stop eating and stand. They follow me out the door to Ted's car.

As soon as I'm back in my room, I call Olive.

"Ted isn't what he seems. Since he's been in my life, my luck is sourer than lemon and pickle juice combined."

"It's like he's cast a spell on you," Olive says.

"Who knows what might happen when he has me in New Hampshire for three weeks?"

"Your mom will be at Lakeside, too, and he wouldn't dare pull any funny business with her around. She'd dump him in a nanosecond if she believed he was hurting you, but keep your guard up."

"Do you think there are evil wizards in real life?"

"No. Do you?"

"I didn't before I met Ted."

CHAPTER 12

I survived graduation. No one made a fuss about Mom being there with Ted, and Ted kept his goofy expressions to himself. He even had the sense not to try to hug me.

Starting the day after the ceremony, Mom dragged me to every store in town to get ready for Lakeside. At least I got to ditch the boot. My foot feels so free and lightweight. According to the doctor, I can start jogging and then build up to running again.

Today, Mom outdoes herself and we come in with bags and bags of clothes. Even Grandpa thinks she has lost it and says, "Enough, Marybeth." He scolded. "Boys don't change their clothes every hour. Rocky might wear the same T-shirt until the smell gets too ripe."

"But I want to make sure he has the right stuff," she says.

"He is my grandson. You bet your bottom, he has the right stuff."

Mom's trips to the mall slowed down after Grandpa's little lecture, and we got the news that he has to have hip surgery. Boom! That's another curveball being thrown directly at my head. Now Mom has to stay here to take care of him, and I'll be stuck at Lakeside all by myself with the devil man.

THE DAY TO leave arrives faster than I wanted it to. I sling my duffle into the trunk of Ted's car, and he throws his suitcase in on top of it. Then, as if we're synchronized dancers, we pivot in unison toward Mom. She's standing next to Grandpa with her arm wrapped in his. She brushes away a few loose tears but keeps her smile pasted in place.

Grandpa calls, "Hey, fellas, you'll have a great time up there. I'm thrilled you're going together." Grandpa must've downed a bottle of cheery pills with his morning OJ; otherwise why would someone facing hip replacement surgery be in such an excellent mood?

I realize I forgot my backpack and head into the house to retrieve it. Grandpa follows me in, maneuvering his walker with tennis balls on the legs as if it's a piece of sports equipment instead of a medical device. He shuffles along, grimacing in pain with each step.

Inside he says, "Rocky, this summer hasn't worked out the way you planned. First, no soccer camp and now Lakeside without Mom, but it'll be far better than you imagine. You're a smart kid. You'll do well."

"But if Mom has to be with you, shouldn't Ted stay here too?"

"He wants to honor their commitment to Lakeside. My hip messed things up. Sorry."

"It's not your fault. I could skip the writing program and help you after the operation." Doing that would help build my case to become Grandpa's chief assistant, so Mom cannot ever make me move away.

But Grandpa doesn't bite and says, "No need for you to miss out. Your mom can take care of everything here."

I hug him, and he squeezes back, reassuring me I'm still top dog as his one and only grandchild.

"You and Ted will have a chance to get better acquainted, and if you need something there, you can ask him." Grandpa pats my head.

No way I'm asking Ted for anything and giving Lord Voldemort even more power over me. I'm just praying I come home in one piece with no more broken bones.

Back outside, Mom pulls me into a tight hug and whispers in my ear, "Call me whenever you can. If you need anything at all, ask Ted."

Again, with the ask Ted. She has no clue how my life might not be safe around him, but like always, when she mentions his name, her blue eyes glow with shiny flecks of gold. I can't wait for her to hear the story I'm going to write about Ted and the bad stuff he does. She will have no choice but to kick him to the curb. My green pen is going for the jugular.

The only plus with Mom being stuck here with Grandpa is that she and Ted will be in different states and can't sneak off to get married.

Like some mothers, she exhibits her superhuman power to read my mind and says, "You're still my number one." Me. Not Ted. For a second, I feel like the boxing match is over, and the ref lifts my arm in victory ending the bout. Still, when Dad was alive, I never considered there was a competition with me sharing Mom with him. Both of them were just mine.

Olive and Max bike up the driveway for this grand farewell. I walk over and slug Max in the gut, which counts as a goodbye, and remind him to memorize all the new techniques he learns from the soccer pro at camp. I'll have a lot to catch up on when I get back and start my training for the new season.

"Hey, I don't want to make varsity without you." he says. Max is a heckuva stand-up guy for sure.

Olive speaks low and says, "So, you and Ted for three weeks. Aren't you the lucky guy? Not."

"If I don't call you from Lakeside when I have phone time, tell my mom because I may be in trouble. You have to be my just-in-case person. Don't abandon me."

"Never, Rocket Man, cross my heart and promise to keep my finger on the 911 speed dial. I'll miss you sooooo much this summer." She uses her gushy voice and flutters her big brown eyes. So funny.

I reply with the other half of our special, secret little routine. "Me too, you."

Then she hands me an envelope and says, "This is a letter for later."

I take it from her hand, feeling a twinge as our fingers touch. Ted breaks up the mood, calling out that it's time to leave. Mom waves goodbye and blows kisses frantically as we pull out of view. I put in my new earbuds to discourage conversation on the way to New Hampshire. I was pumped Mom gave them to me as a going-away present until she handed the same package to Ted. It made my knees go weak that she hadn't picked them out specially for me. Still, they are Bluetooth with awesome bass, and I love them.

After driving a half hour, Ted takes a hand off the wheel and waves it in front of my face. I pull out one bud to listen. "Tell me if you have to pee or barf, and we'll stop," he says.

"Uh-huh," I reply.

I'm about to replace the earbud when he says, "Did you know Lakeside Academy is a famous boarding school during the year? The writing program is their summer gig."

"Nope."

"And did you know this writing program is as fierce as any championship soccer match?"

How could that be? A bunch of high school students writing stories doesn't strike me as a cutthroat group.

Ted continues, "I wrote plays in competitions in high school. I was once up for a state prize, and a kid found my script and copied some of my best lines. They accepted his play for performance, but not mine. He was a thief, but I couldn't prove it."

"That's sick."

"I lost out on a big scholarship to a drama program because of that guy. So just saying, watch your back."

That warning seems over-the-top for a writing camp. I think these strange comments are his way of baiting a fishhook and waiting for me to bite. He's gonna have to wait forever. The rest of the drive passes in silence. I listen to my playlist, thinking about the type of kids who will be at Lakeside.

The scenery begins to get more rural with thick forest on either side of a twisty road. I swallow to pop my ears as we climb higher into the mountains. It's pretty remote here. Before long, a wooden sign with letters made of birch branches appears on the right: Lakeside Academy. Ted pulls onto a dirt road, and we bounce along, listening to the tires crunch on the sparse gravel until we reach an area with parked cars. This place reminds me of the state parks Dad took me to when we went camping.

When I step out of the car, I do a couple of knee bends to loosen up the kinks after the long ride. As Ted pops the trunk, a loud screech overhead forces my eyes upward. A bird with an unsettling, nasty squawk circles us, and it gets louder when it's right above me. Plop! Bird poop runs down from my forehead to my cheek.

"Disgusting! Crappola," I say. "That bird was gunning for me."

"I've got wipes in the console," Ted says. "It's unusual for a bird to make a direct hit. A guy I knew at college—"

Ted stops short, and his eyes go wide. It seems that whatever he was going to say startled him, and he pulled it back. When he opens his mouth again, he still sounds confused. "Er...no, I'm mixing that up with something I read in a book," and then he busies himself with opening the wipes. Luckily, no one is around to watch this spectacle, so I let him clean me off because I can't see where the stuff is. I might miss a spot, and I don't want to start the program known as the bird-poop kid.

"Did you get it all?" I ask.

"Sure did."

"Do I smell?" This gunk stinks. A bird once dive-bombed Dad, and he said the odor made him gag. I guess I inherited the bird-poop-target gene from him.

Ted puts his nose to my face and hair and announces, "Like a rose garden. No, seriously, you're fine."

I am not fine. A random bird attacks me and leaves him alone—and so it begins. For three weeks, Ted will have many opportunities to create havoc in my life.

PART 2:

LAKESIDE ARTS AND WRITING PROGRAM

CHAPTER 13

Ted and I follow the signs to registration and wind up at a cleared area facing an enormous log cabin. That building could be straight out of pioneer days with old-timey people inside in long dresses and fur frontier hats, churning butter or making cider. I put my duffle down for a second to give my arm a rest.

"You can handle it from here," Ted says, pointing to tables with signs A-H, I-P, and Q-Z. "I have to report to the office." He moves in closer, and my body shrinks into itself as I step backward to avoid the hug he might be crazy enough to try to land on me. And I end up tumbling over my bag.

Eyeballing me with his steaming tar-colored eyes, he stretches out his hand to help me up, but I don't trust him and jump to my feet on my own power.

"Are you okay?" he asks.

"Yup," I reply. Another fall courtesy of Ted. This makes number three. The first one was on Tucker's auditorium steps, the second on the soccer field, and now this. For a coordinated kid, I have become accident prone since I met Ted. I go stand in the A-H line and hope not too many people noticed my clumsy arrival.

When it's my turn, the girl behind the table asks, "Name?"

"Casson."

"Okay, Casson, you're assigned to Cabin 4, down the path to the left. Wear this name tag until we know who you are."

I examine the name tag, and the word RONALD in over-sized capital letters causes an inner groan to bellow in the back of my throat. I've been Rocky since first grade, when Dad gifted me with the best nickname ever because I didn't want to be called Junior anymore.

"Um...um...can you tell me who my workshop leader is?" I ask the girl.

"It's in your packet. Next!" Her loud voice signals I should move on. I gather up the lanyard and a big white envelope with my instructions and follow the signs to Cabin 4.

Perched on a low branch on the path, a bird makes its presence known. I swear it looks just like the one who bombed me earlier. If I didn't know better, it could be smiling.

I'm not taking any chances. I glare at the winged creature with my eyebrows pinched together in a stern warning and say, "Do I look like your toilet, birdie?" Then I hurry away before he targets me again.

A kid about eighteen or so is sitting outside the cabin door reading a comic book. He looks up and asks, "Name?"

"Rocky Casson."

He checks his list and says, "You mean Ronald. Got you. I'm Jono, your take-no-prisoners cabin leader, which is not the same thing as a counselor. There are no babies here, and I'm not your mama. I sleep over there." He points to a tent nearby. "And I keep a lookout for any ninth-grade funny business."

He points his fingers at his eyes and then at me in the classic I'm-watching-you motion. "If you have questions, you know where I am." With that, he returns to his reading.

I open the cabin door. Two guys are sitting on the bottom of one of the bunk beds with sketch pads on their laps. Obvs, they're in the arts part of the program.

The big blond kid with a few rows of freckles under his pale blue eyes smiles at me and says, "Pick your bed. Your shelf and cubby are over there." He points to a corner of the room. "I'm Luke. This is my brother, Yosh."

He clucks his tongue. I think he is waiting for a comment or question about how it's possible for him to be brothers with an Asian kid. Yosh giggles, and I suspect this is some joke the two of them cooked up to test my reaction.

I bet they expect me to say they can't possibly be brothers, or they want me to laugh at their weird attempt at humor. I ignore the trap and say, "Hi, Yosh."

Their eyes zero in on me, which makes me squirmy. I start to check myself out, stopping at my zipper in case that's the problem.

"What's your name?" Yosh asks.

"Oh, sorry. I'm Rocky." No one asks if I'm named after the famous boxer, which is the usual next line.

I open my duffle and start to unpack. It goes well until I pull out one can of bug spray after another. *Moooommm*, I scream in my head, *what did you do?* There are six of them. I'm not putting them all on my shelf and getting labeled a wuss about flying or crawling creatures. I keep one out and shove the rest of the death-to-bugs stuff back into my bag.

Then, I find way too many tubes of sunscreen. Ha, Mom, and you were the one to always scold Dad about overdoing things like when he bought twenty different hair products for an experiment.

I expect there will be a dozen bottles of Purell, but there aren't any. Must have slipped her mind.

A man and woman walk in. They have the same dark, straight hair like Yosh and the man is just as thin. Except for the fact the man is older, he and Yosh could be brothers. The couple makes a slight bow toward me. I'm not sure what the correct response is, so I just say hi. The man walks over and kisses Luke on the top of his head and says, "Enough drawing, boys. Walk us to the car. We have to get home."

"In a sec, Papa," Luke says, as he attacks the paper with his charcoal pencil. "I have to finish something."

"Okay. Mama and I will wait outside for you and Yoshiki."

They are brothers, for real. If this was in English class, Ms. Rotterdam would ask the author, "What's the backstory here?" But I don't like it when people get into my business, so I'm not going there.

Yosh introduces me to his parents. "Hey, this is Rocky."

"Hi, Rocky, like the prizefighter?" his dad asks, falling into the typical response when people hear my name. I remind them of Rocky Marciano, the undefeated heavyweight champ from Massachusetts and also the Rocky from the movies.

"Yup, like the famous boxer." I raise my fists in a fighting stance for good visual effect.

"Hey, Rocky, that's a great pose," Luke says. "Can I draw you after our 'rents hit the road?"

"Sure. Where did you guys put your suitcases after you unpacked?" I ask.

The mom answers, "Near the cabin door. Jono will put them in storage until the program ends."

"Thanks."

The four of them leave. I deposit my duffle by the front door. Back in the room, I climb up to the top bunk and sort out my notebooks, pens, and flashlight. I should get my butt in gear right away and start writing, but a series of knocks prevents that. It better not be Ted coming to check up on me. I'd rather eat a bowl of mashed green peas than have to introduce him as the man who wants to marry my mom. I ignore the knocks, as sweat rivers flow from my pits, even though I used a ton of deodorant this morning.

More knocks, but this time they're accompanied by a woman's voice saying, "Are you all decent? Mother here."

Whew. Not Ted. I answer, "Yes. Come in."

A dude with serious movie-star looks walks in. His deep brown eyes check out the room and land on me. He opens his mouth to reveal bright, white teeth that are so straight he must have great tooth genes or the best orthodontist in the world. His pink polo stands out against his dark skin. Compared to him, I'm a skinny scarecrow with straggly hair. Without thinking, my hand brushes the mop off my face, even though I know it will soon be back on my forehead without any gel to glue it in place. No gel. That's the one thing Mom forgot to pack. Maybe I can trade some sunscreen for hair gel, although this guy won't have any. He doesn't need any help for his hair.

"So, I guess this bottom bed is mine," the kid says.

I nod.

"I'm Malik, and this is my mother," he says and takes out a notebook and pens from his backpack, which he shoves under the bed.

His mom rushes to retrieve it and brush the dust off. "Honey-pie, it will get so dirty under there. I'll unpack it after I finish with your suitcase." His mom opens the bright red bag and arranges his clothes in neat piles with the folds facing out. Compared to Malik's shelves, everyone else's looks like a tornado was in charge of the organization, but then again, Malik might be the only one who had his mother arrange things for him.

Malik's mom continues to work, interrupting him with occasional questions about where she should put things. He answers her but never gets up to help, and what's most surprising is she never asks him to.

I let my head hang down over Malik's bed and say, "Hey, I'm Rocky from Massachusetts."

He says, "Manhattan."

Yosh and Luke return and introduce themselves to Malik. It turns out the brothers live in downtown Boston near the Garden where the Celtics play. They're both going to be freshmen like me, but they don't go to the same high school, which is odd. All the sibs I know go to the same school.

Malik's mom says, "Sugar, I'm done. Do you need anything else?"

Holy moly, who is this woman? I bet this guy doesn't load the dishwasher or take out the trash at home. His family must hire someone to do his chores.

"No. You can go." Malik doesn't even get off his butt to hug her. His mom gives him a little kiss on the cheek.

She asks, "Don't you want to come out and say goodbye to Dad and your brothers?"

"And disturb them while they're tossing around their precious football? Not a good idea."

His mom looks at me and explains. "They're always practicing football. That's what Malik means."

"Sounds like fun," I say.

"Then why don't you play with them?" Malik snarks but doesn't take his eyes off his paper.

Whoa, what's that all about? Why did he burn me? This dude may be trouble.

His mom says, "I'll tell them you said goodbye and to have a nice summer."

"Sure," Malik responds and returns to his writing, as if he has to get something on paper fast before he loses his idea. A few times that happened to me, and I had to write something immediately and was almost late for school.

Malik's mom waves and leaves.

I remove the nametag from the plastic holder on my lanyard, black out the word *Ronald* and write ROCKY above it. Then I open the registration packet. I got Ms. Williams! Ms. Rotterdam must have clout here. She got me into Williams's group *and* also managed to wrangle a job for Ted.

I lean my head over the edge of the bed again, and say, "Hey, Malik, who did you get for workshop leader?"

"The one and only Althea Williams. Nothing but the best for me," he says, as if there was no other possibility.

"Me too."

Malik's face changes, and he looks like his dog just died. Is he crazy enough to think he'd be the only person in her group?

He slaps on a fake grin and says, "Too bad we're in the same group. Hope you won't take it personal when I cut you to shreds in the workshop. I plan on taking the top prize for rising ninth graders home."

"Shreds? I doubt that," I respond. That's not happening. Going to LA is too important to me.

Malik says matter-of-factly, "This program will make my career. Writing is in my bones, everyone tells me."

"Game on," I say.

"You must've written an excellent story to be here," Yosh says, glancing up from his sketch pad for a minute and studying Malik's changing expressions. OMG, he's using Malik as a model.

"I did write a brilliant story, and the governor thought so too," Malik replies.

That guy needs humblizing, and I'm making that my job.

CHAPTER 14

Clang! Clang! My eardrums shudder as an earthquake rattles my brain. I turn to move away from the awful racket. *Thwap!* Down I go, smacking my back against Yosh's bedframe on my way to the floor. Stunned. I don't move.

"Hey, are you all right?" Yosh asks.

Luke jumps down and offers me his hand. I grab it and push through the pain to stand.

Once I'm upright, I say, "I'm fine. Ha. Ha. Can you believe I forgot I was sleeping in a top bunk?"

Luke asks, "Did you get hurt? Should we take you to the infirmary?"

"Nah." That's a lie, because my back is killing me, but I can't risk missing the first workshop. That would give Malik a head start in this hand-to-hand—I mean pen-to-pen—combat. I glance in Malik's direction. The dude says nothing, but at least he isn't laughing at me.

"That was seriously the worst wake-up noise ever," I say.

"Jono's a whack job to use cymbals. Thinks he's so funny. Frightening, huh?" Yosh says.

I wash up and get dressed in slow-mo because my back feels bruised and battered. I think this might be equal to how much pain Grandpa was in with his bum hip.

Inside the log cabin, I spot Ted sitting with some other adults. He waves at me, and I ignore him and head for my table. Did Ted already forget the promise to maintain a low profile? Mom isn't around to remind him, so he must think he can get away with anything.

Malik asks, "Who is that guy?"

"Who?" I pretend I have no idea who he's talking about so he'll drop his questions, and I won't have to acknowledge Ted.

Malik doesn't comply and continues, "The guy with the tool belt," he explains.

"Just a friend of my mom's from Milton who's working here." Using the word friend about Ted makes me shiver. It would be more accurate to introduce him as a witch whose job is to torment me.

Then I connect the dots. Ted warned me to watch my back and pretended it was about the competitive kids here, and wham, I destroy my back this morning. Coincidence? I think not. This will be added to my growing list of reasons Mom can't marry Ted.

After breakfast, Malik and I walk to the grove for our workshop. I'm glad I was assigned morning sessions so my afternoons are free for swimming or writing.

My first step into the grove transports me into a world of beauty. Pine trees circle the area so their branches form a roof overhead that allows just a sliver of sun to peek through. There are already kids there, and I join them on the ground, which is blanketed in soft pine needles. I lower myself gingerly to protect my back.

I check around for Malik, expecting he'd be sitting next to me, only to discover he's already chatting with Ms. Williams as if they've been buds forever. She smiles at Malik with bright red lips while he shows her something in his notebook.

Ms. Williams could be a queen. She's majestic in a robe of

blue and green stripes, held together with a wide sash. She wears huge gold earrings that dangle against her brown skin and put me in a hypnotic trance. Her head is shaved, but she sure doesn't resemble any old bald man.

I'm surprised at how much my powers of observation have improved since Ms. Rotterdam's assignment to make us aware of our surroundings. For two weeks, we had to keep notebooks in our pockets so we could jot down details about the people we came into contact with. Once, I got caught staring too long at the cashier in the supermarket, and she shot me a nasty look. I averted my eyes before she called the cops and reported me as a stalker.

Ms. Williams's chin rises, propelled by her laughter, which echoes through the trees. Malik doesn't seem like the humorous type. He gives off more of a serious vibe. He may be beyond handsome, but I don't think he has much of a sense of humor. I'd love to get Malik together with the nonstop joker Max just to annoy him.

The first workshop didn't even start yet, and already I'm losing ground to Malik. Getting the top prize will be a hefty challenge with this guy sopping up all Ms. Williams's attention.

When they finish talking, Malik joins us. The girls in the workshop can't stop gawking at him like they've never seen someone so perfect. Even in this heat, his clothes are crisp and the light blue shirt and khaki shorts accentuate the rich color of his skin. My eyes drop to my pale legs, and I decide to ditch the sunscreen from now on.

Ms. Williams begins. "Welcome, authors, to Lakeside. Here in the majestic mountains of New Hampshire, you will scale the heights of creative writing. I'll be your guide on this exquisite journey. Please call me Althea."

She strolls through the grove while she speaks, making her belt-thing swish around her. Ms. Williams, I mean Althea, continues, "There will be assignments, writing prompts, craft-building projects, and public readings."

Malik raises his hand.

"No need to raise hands, Malik. We're informal here among the picturesque pines."

She knows his name already!

"Althea," he says, "can you tell us more about the top prize?"

"Of course I can. At the end of this program, one person in each grade level will receive a monetary award and a trip for two to the national event in Los Angeles."

"And who picks the winner?" Malik asks, with a sly grin that makes me think he already knows the answer but is asking for our benefit.

Althea dazzles him with her own glowing smile. "That would be me, the best-selling author." She laughs, and we join her.

Next, she has us go around in a circle and introduce ourselves. When Malik speaks, the girls drool, but Malik seems not to notice they exist. He mentions the name of his school, and Althea responds with the words "creme de la crème." That sounds like Klingon to me, though Althea seems super impressed with his school.

When the workshop ends, Althea gives us a form to fill out with details about one of our main characters. No sweat. My main character DET is easy to write about. I know him quite well. I slip the sheet into my notebook.

The girls crowd around Malik and pepper him with questions, trying to hold his attention.

Another guy in our workshop, a kid named JJ, stands next to me as the scene unfolds and says, "These girls can't believe someone like Malik even exists, just like you can't imagine a fish on a bicycle."

I grin and say, "My guess is they never met an actual Prince Charming before. He's straight out of a Disney movie."

"You're right, but if he's P.C., that would make me the toad in the movie," JJ says and bumps me with his shoulder.

Malik breaks away from his fan club, and we walk to lunch. In a loud voice so everyone can hear, he says, "I already told my parents to buy my ticket for Los Angeles."

The dude has no shame, but I have to admit he is laser focused, and it won't be easy to beat him. I'll have to step up my game if I want to go to Los Angeles for Dad and me.

CHAPTER 15

That night at dinner, all the kids chow down fast, as if gobbling their food will make eight o'clock come sooner. The hour arrives in its own sweet time, and everyone descends on the office to retrieve their cell phones. Lakeside has a no-cell rule, claiming that disconnecting from distractions helps to rev up our creativity. But holding this baby in my hand again is a glorious reunion.

Everyone scatters like raccoons in the light to find some privacy. I settle on a faraway spot so no eavesdroppers will skulk nearby. With one ring, Olive answers.

"How are you? What's Ted up to?" The words fly out of her as if they have been cooped up inside for a long time, ready to make a run for it as soon as escape is possible.

"I'm okay now."

"What do you mean *now*? That doesn't sound good." Her worried tone reminds me of Mom's when she was in extreme hovering mode after Dad died.

"I fell out of the top bunk," I explain.

She laughs. "Picturing you toppling down is a little funny."

"I hurt my back. The strange thing is that the day before, Ted told me to 'watch my back.'"

"Do you think he's predicting your future?"

"I think he's creating my future. He might be a real-life Draco."

"Then if he offers you a drink, refuse! It could be a tall frosty glass of frog's eye, skin of a snake and bat's wing."

Her laughter is deafening. She's playing with me. An image of Ted cooking up a mystery potion is humorous, but I'm rattled.

"And there's a bird poop story, too." That sends her over the edge giggling, which I should've predicted. Bird poop is hilarious unless it's dripping down *your* face. I wait for her to recover.

"Are you sure that wasn't a dream?" she asks.

"You can't dream about being covered in that stinky slime."

"Poor guy. Listen, my mom is taking me to Salem this weekend to research witches. Do you remember when we had the unit on the witches' hysteria there? Not all the people who were hanged were women. They accused a few men of being possessed. I'll try to dig up some useful information for you."

"Good idea," I say, grateful as ever for her help.

We hang up. I should have told her about Malik and how I now have to watch myself around him too. I feel like he and Ted are playing with me like I'm in a game of Monkey in the Middle. I'm the one being shoved around, getting my brains whipped up into disgusting gray matter cream.

The next call is to Mom. "Hi, Mom, how's Grandpa doing?"

She gives me the deets of the operation while I swat mosquitoes filling their bellies with my blood. I regret not using the bug spray tonight.

"Mom, if Grandpa needs more help, I could come home." Although if I leave now, it will cost me my chance for the L.A. trip. Still, I have to take advantage of every opportunity to lay the foundation for Plan B.

"Such a sweet offer. We're managing fine. I'm not going into the office for a while."

I describe spectacular Ms. Williams and my roommates, omitting any comments about Malik's outrageous attitude.

"How's your writing going?" Mom asks.

"Not bad," I say. "I'm starting a brand-new story."

"What's it about?"

"I'll let you read it when I'm finished. It has a very realistic plot."

At nine o'clock, the kids line up like prison inmates, to return their phones. From everyone's faces, you'd think we were giving up a body part.

Back in the cabin, I start my assignment and list Ted's, I mean DET's, qualities:

Sneaky

Trickster

Black devil's beard and dark tar-like eyes that turn to yellow when he uses his evil powers.

A horrible cackle that signals imminent disaster.

And on I go, filling out the entire form describing Ted, aka DET. It's a piece of cake.

THE NEXT MORNING, Jono replaces his cymbals with a drum. What a jerk. But I remember I'm on a top bunk even before I open my eyes. I look around my bed for my homework from last night. I remember conking out before I could put it in my folder. I ease myself off the bed, guarding against another crash to the floor and hunt for the missing form.

"What are you searching for?" Yosh asks, poking his head out of his T-shirt.

"My assignment for today," I answer. "It's a form that—"

"You mean this?" Malik waves the paper he has been reading.

I snatch it from his hand. "Where did you get that?"

"Calm down, man. It landed on my pillow. I thought you wanted me to read it."

"You thought wrong," I say. Sharing my paper with a guy who wants to skunk me into oblivion would be like giving the opposing team your game plan. I don't trust him.

IN THE WORKSHOP, Althea calls on Malik first to present his character's description. The girls hang on his every word as if each one is a gift from God. Chloe shimmies her butt close to him until their knees touch. Malik reads through his list, unaware of the girl moving in on him.

I'm stunned as he describes a spooky archduke with dark thick eyebrows that almost cover his black eyes which turn to green when he uses his power. He copied that off of me!

JJ, who's become a writing pal, whispers, "Are you all right? You look pale. Are you going to pass out?"

"I'm...I'm fine," I say. Now when I get called on, everyone will think I'm a copycat. What Malik wrote is practically the same as my descriptions. It can't be a coincidence.

Althea opens the discussion on Malik's description, and the girls bubble over as if it's pure perfection. They can't find one teeny bit of criticism for him. That must be the fate of all hot guys.

I'm up next. I describe DET, the star of my story, but omit the tar color of his eyes that turn yellow so it won't be too similar to Malik's character.

For me, Isabelle and Chloe throw out some critical comments, which Chloe tops off with the question I was dreading. "Did you channel Malik when you wrote this? Sounds like you might've copied."

"No. Maybe he channeled me," I say.

Chloe rolls her eyes. "I really doubt that. Malik is too amazing."

Althea takes over the critique and surprises me with positive comments never mentioning how alike Malik's and my descriptions are. She says, "Great potential, Rocky. You should add more dark magic to your character, which will make him more mysterious and spice up the story."

Whew! No accusations of plagiarism, which Ms. Rotterdam says is the kiss of death for a would-be author.

On our way to lunch, I ask Malik whether his vile archduke always had eyes that changed color or if that's something new he added.

He says, "No, that was in my original story. The archduke is a combination hero and villain, but I'm not saying more. Don't want to give you any ideas. This story will take me all the way to the main event in L.A."

Okay, I'll give him the benefit of the doubt that he isn't a cheater and a jerk—only just a jerk.

I enter the log cabin, and Ted's right by the door, in my face. I can't avoid him. He says, "Heard you fell from the top bunk the other night."

"Who told you?" I ask.

"Jono, your cabin leader."

I'm not offering Ted the satisfaction that I hurt my back, just like he warned me.

Then the convo takes a twisted turn. "Rocky, should you and I wear suits at the wedding?"

Wedding! Oh, no. Time may be running out.

"Did you decide on a date?" I gulp after each word and say a silent prayer that I still have time.

"Not yet. We're in the planning stage, deciding how many

of our friends and family we will invite. Eloping is not for us like—"

Again, he stops talking midsentence, and his neck reddens. The color travels to his face, and he mutters something incoherent, as if he lost track of what he was gonna say. He seems befuddled.

When he regains his composure, he says, "Oh, I don't mean there's anything wrong with eloping, it's just that we decided..."

His sentence drifts into the air incomplete, and he changes the subject, saying,

"Someone told me there's a guy in your group who might be competition for you, but I have a hunch you'll beat him."

OMG, another of Ted's hunches. Is he planning to hex Malik, too?

I don't want to win if it's because of Ted's dirty deeds. Dad would never knee-cap an opponent, and he, for sure, wouldn't approve if I did.

CHAPTER 16

A few days later, heading to our cabin after lunch, Yosh says, "It's boiling out. Let's go to the lake this afternoon."

"I'm in," Luke replies, which is no surprise. Unlike Malik, who doesn't like his siblings much, these brothers seem joined at the hip.

"Do you guys want to swim out to the raft?" I ask, bringing up the rear. The raft is cool. It's tied to the end of the dock and bobs on the water, but most of the time, the older kids hog it. If I go with these guys, we can commandeer our own section.

Yosh opens the door to our room and jumps backward, crashing into Malik, who's right behind him.

Malik shoves him forward, annoyed, "What the heck, Yoshiki?"

Once we're all inside, it's clear what startled Yosh. Our clothes are in a big heap in the middle of the floor.

"Why would anyone do this?" Yosh asks, stepping over a small mountain of boxers, pjs, and T-shirts.

Luke stares at the mess. "More important, who did this?" He leans over to pick up a piece of paper sitting on top of the pile and drops it as if it burns his skin. "It's wet. What if it's not water? You couldn't get me to touch that again."

The guys turn into motionless statues, so I step forward and take the half sheet of notebook paper, ready to make a mad dash to the bathroom to scrub my hands if the liquid isn't harmless. I take a whiff. Water. Someone is trying to freak us out.

I read the note. "Courtesy of your official prankster!"

"Let me see that," Luke says, snatching it from my hand. "Green ink. Familiar much, Rocky?" Luke shakes the paper in front of my face.

"I didn't write that," I insist.

"It's printed in small letters like you do," Luke says.

Malik stretches his leg over the pile to get to his bed. He sits, pulling his feet in close so no part of him touches the clothes. He says, "You could pretend to be brave because you knew exactly what that liquid is."

"How would I know?"

"Duh? I can't believe you're so dumb and that you think we're dumb. You had plenty of time for a quick run to the cabin when you stayed back to talk to the tool belt guy before lunch. You could've snuck back here to pull this dumb stunt, since everyone's things are dumped on the floor, except yours," Malik says.

Word echo, Malik, can you say "dumb" enough? But I run my eyes over my shelves and he's right. Whoever did this left my stuff untouched.

Luke scowls. "Why would you do that, man?"

"I did *not* do this," I protest.

"So how come your clothes are still in the cubbies?" Yosh asks.

"I don't know," I repeat, losing the battle to maintain my inner calm so my body doesn't tremble with anger. This has to be Ted's handiwork because he knows how I make my letters and that I always use a green pen. Why would he do this and pin it on me?

"I don't know why my stuff isn't in the pile. Honestly. I'll help put things away."

"You do that," Malik says, "and do a good job. Luke, Yosh, let's leave this bonehead so he can set things right. To the lake."

"What! I said I'd help. I didn't say I'd do the whole thing," I call after them as they grab their bathing suits from the clothes heap and disappear, leaving me alone to grapple with this mess.

I put the damp items to the side to dry and start folding clothes. I pay close attention to making sure that all Malik's embroidered whales on his polos are swimming in the same direction, just like his mother did when she unpacked for him. He doesn't own anything with an Old Navy label. Most of his clothes are brands that are new to me, probably high-end. Malik is so rich.

When I finish, I'm sweaty so I head for the shower. By the time I return, the guys are back, but no one speaks to me or even says thanks for cleaning up.

This little horror show has left me ostracized from my roommates. I'll pay Ted back with the same green pen he used. Before I continue my "bury Ted" story, I dig out my list of why Mom can't marry Ted and add his latest sin.

REASONS NOT TO MARRY TED

1. Does Mom know this guy, except for doing his taxes?
2. His tiny, pointy beard and bushy eyebrows in continual motion.
3. Gives unwanted soccer advice.
4. Suitcase?
5. He made me fall out of the top bunk.
6. Bird poop??????

7. He pranked my roommates and left me to take the blame.

LATER THAT NIGHT during phone time, I call Mom. She third-degrees me about my foot and reminds me in her strictest voice not to kick any balls until I get home.

"Rocky, Ted's coming to Milton soon for a day, so if you need anything, he can bring it back for you."

What I need is to be certain they don't run off and get married.

"I have a question."

"Ask anything," she says. "No more secrets between us. I promised." When Dad died, she didn't tell me the truth about what happened to him. When I finally found out, she promised she would never break our trust bond again.

"Would you get married while I'm here at Lakeside?"

"I can't have a wedding without my best man."

"Best what?" I ask.

"Best man. I need you to stand beside me. This is an enormous step for both of us."

"Yes, it is. Are you sure you've thought this through?" This is a role reversal where I sound like the responsible parent trying to convince their kid they're not ready to make such a momentous decision.

She chuckles. "I'm lucky there are three exceptional men in my life. Ted's eager to be your friend. He's scared you might not like him."

That's the funniest thing she's said in a long, long time. What a riot! He's scared of me? Boy, he has succeeded in acing his course in brainwashing. Mom's so gullible where he's concerned.

"Maybe I'm scared of him. Did you ever consider that? Do you notice how his hunches about me wind up coming true? You have to admit that's weird."

"It's because he's smart with a real talent for analyzing situations. Listen, there's not much more I can say to convince you that having Ted in our lives is a good thing. But I promise that our life will only get better after we're married. Remember, Dad used to say a person has to take some risks or they will never succeed. This is a risk worth taking."

Quoting Dad usually shuts me up, but this time is different. I'm still going after Ted. I say, "Do you think Ted sometimes says crazy stuff, especially to me?"

"Ted isn't experienced around kids and gets awkward at times." Once again, Mom takes his side. She has moved out of my corner and into Ted's. It's like she's his second at a boxing match, passing him the bottle of water and towel instead of me.

"Mom, I've got to go so I can call Olive before we have to turn in our phones."

"Okay. Take care of yourself, Love you, sweetheart," she says.

I press Olive's speed dial.

"Hey, Olive. So, was the sky crowded with people riding their broomsticks in Salem?" I joke.

"No recent information about witches and wizards. Everything there goes back to the 1600s. I came up with another idea. You need to do more investigating. Search Ted's things. Remember when you snooped around your mom's room and came across a big clue that finally led you to discovering the truth about your dad?"

"What am I supposed to be looking for?"

"Anything suspicious."

CHAPTER 17

The next morning, the guys are still frosty and avoid me as if I've got the plague. They leave for breakfast before I'm even dressed, and to add to today's bad start, Ted's lurking outside the log cabin.

"Low profile, Ted, remember?" I remind him, as I brush past. I can't listen to his jibber-jabber this morning. First chance I get I'm going to search his room for a link to the prank. Maybe he took a trophy.

At the table, Malik announces, "I came up with the best title for my story." His arm stretches behind him as he pretends to pat himself on the back.

"Want to hear it?" he asks.

"Yup," I say.

Malik rises out of his seat and leans across the table to whisper so only Yoshiki and Luke can hear him, cutting me out. Boy, that stings.

Yosh snorts his milk, and Luke doubles over, almost sending his butt to the floor. Must've been a good joke, but I bet it had nothing to do with his story and was a hit on me.

For the rest of the meal, I study my plate as my fork pushes the food around to look like I'm eating. My appetite has disappeared. I have to get back into the circle because A, I didn't do anything to these guys and B, being shut out is brutal.

When breakfast is over, I dog Malik all the way to the grove, even when he shifts speed to try to shake me. I say, "I swear, Malik, I'm no prankster," once again, claiming my innocence.

Finally, Malik slow-turns and acknowledges my existence. "Okay, I can be a magnanimous guy. I'll accept you didn't do it, but you only get one benefit of the doubt from me."

"Great, that's all I need." I lift my fist for a bump and say, "Happy to own a get-out-of-jail free card."

Malik completes the fist bump, and I follow with the hand explosion, but his fist doesn't explode. Oh, well, better than nothing.

Then Malik offers to speak to the brothers for me and fix things with them too. "Enough of this," he says, "I have to concentrate on writing. I don't have time for anything else."

"Yup. Fine with me. Thanks."

We sit on the ground and watch Althea take some papers from her bag. Seeing her bright smile always lifts my spirits, and today is no exception. Her silver scarf shimmers around her neck, and I try to count the number of bracelets stacked on her arm from her wrist to elbow, but give up when she starts the workshop.

She says, "I have some morning inspiration for you. Maya Angelou, a renowned poet, memoirist, and a woman of uncommon intelligence wrote these words: 'Words mean more than what is set down on paper. It takes the human voice to infuse them with deeper meaning.' This Thursday evening, you will infuse your work in your own voice. You will read the regional award-winning stories that brought you to Lakeside. Polish up those beauties. I'm assigning critique partners for this: Isabelle and JJ, Malik and Rocky, Chloe and Crystal."

Has this woman lost her mind? Even though Malik's talking

to me now, working with him will be torture. He'll hate anything I write, and I'll have to suck up to him with glowing comments because that's what he expects. Any of the girls would have been delirious to be partners with him.

The critique pairs break away to find private places to work. Malik motions to me with a bent finger to follow him and leads me from the grove to a denser part of the woods.

We sit and take out our papers. He says, "I have to be far away from those girls. They won't let me work."

"They're crushing on you, man. Don't you like any of them?"

"Sure, I do, but I have no time for them. I need to keep my focus. There's a lot at stake for me. Winning will prove I'm talented."

"Prove to who?"

"To my dad. The girls keep trying to distract me. I deal with this at school all the time, and I promised myself to keep the girls far away from me up here."

I guess being smart and handsome has some drawbacks, but we have one thing in common: we're trying to win the prize for our dads.

We fall into silence as we write. Only the fluttering birds' wings and the scratching paws of squirrels scurrying up the tree trunks interrupt the peacefulness. After I reread my story, I check my watch and realize there's still an hour until lunch, which is more than enough time to search Ted's room while everyone's still at work.

I put my notebook and pen into my backpack and say, "Malik, my stomach is gnarly. Got to go back to the cabin. We can do the critiques later."

He's so immersed in his work that he merely grunts something similar to "okay." At least I'm taking it as an okay.

I fling my backpack over one shoulder and take off at a

normal, unsuspicious pace. The staff area is off behind a hill so they won't be bothered by noisy kids when they're off duty.

There's a row of tiny cabins, each marked with the name of the occupant so it's easy to find Ted's. I'm surprised Mr. Electronic Lock has left his door unbolted so anyone can walk right in. I was prepared to climb through a window, which I've done before at my old house in Whitman and consider myself an accomplished break-in artist.

Ted's room is small but neat. Mom must love the neat part of him. She was always cleaning up after Dad, especially after he had been lying on the sofa for days, watching old movies and surrounded by empty candy wrappers, soda cans, and half-eaten apples.

On a quick scan of his room, I note there are no jars of dead animals or bugs waiting to be cooked up into a deadly potion. I can check that off the list. I crouch to look under the bed. Work boots, sneakers, and an enormous book. This might be his secret witches' handbook, which would be the smoking gun to prove to Mom who we're dealing with.

Once again, I strike out. The title of the book is *The Complete Guide to Soccer* and it has lots of sticky notes marking many of the pages. Why would he be reading this, unless he's devising new ways to interfere with my soccer game?

I put the book back and open his drawers, feeling like a creepster to be searching through his underwear and socks. My skin prickles as if little acupuncture needles are covering my arms. I know I shouldn't be doing this, but there's no choice.

In his T-shirt drawer, the red one on the top of the pile makes me fight for my next breath. Dad had the same exact shirt from his college, which he only wore to the beach and never washed, so it always smelled salty. He insisted the washing machine would wear it out too fast and there were too many memories in the threads.

My heart pings when I see that logo again. I run my fingers over it, and I'm about to pull it out to inspect it when voices come through the raised window. I peek out. Ted and Althea are heading this way. A hot anger burns in my chest seeing them together, probably talking about me. He'd better not mention anything about marrying my mother. I don't want my mixed-up life put on display at Lakeside.

I climb out of the back window, lower myself to the ground, and slither army-style on my belly until I'm in the clear. Then I stand and race toward a cluster of trees for cover.

Ted's raspy cackle rides the sound waves through the air. "Althea, check your cabin. My door is wide open. Someone's been inside."

I take off like Usain Bolt and don't slow down until the log cabin is in sight. Miraculously, my healing foot cooperated. No pain, not even a twinge. I stop, double over and clutch my knees, waiting for the banging in my chest to subside. A close call for sure.

Suddenly, a frightening thought slithers into my brain. This construction dude might have installed hidden cameras in his room. I never checked for those. What a cruddy detective I'd make. Too late now.

CHAPTER 18

W hen the night of the public readings arrives, Ted still
hasn't dropped the hammer on me as the intruder, so I
dodged that bullet. Maybe I do have some talent for being a top
detective, or maybe my luck has simply improved.

I've been working on my writing nonstop for hours, and I'm
surprised my hand didn't fall off. Tonight is the first step to
nailing down my dream trip to Los Angeles and a tour of the
men's soccer training facility.

In case Dad knows what's happening in my life, I say inside
my head, *Dad, if you can hear me, keep your fingers crossed and
put in a good word for me with you-know-who. I've got a shot at
this if I can outperform Malik.*

We return to the cabin after dinner to change clothes, and I
study Malik's every move as he gets ready because he has
fashion sense, and I don't. He puts on a button-down shirt with
a small patch of an open-mouth, beady-eyed tiger on the front. I
don't own anything with a little animal on it, so I just wear my
plain blue-and-green plaid shirt.

Malik chooses khaki cargo shorts, which surprises me
because I would have thought it would be a jeans night. I put on
shorts too, but I'm outgunned by his bright red canvas slip-ons,
which I've never seen on him before. I can't imitate that, so I

lace up my last year's Nikes and hope no one does a Malik-Rocky clothes comparison.

"Hey, man, cool shoes," I say.

"I wear them for competitions. They bring me luck, as if I need it. Rocky, no crying at the reading if I get the most applause." He laughs.

Trash talking in a writing contest is hilarious. I have experience dishing verbal slaps on the soccer field, so I know how to serve Malik up a heaping taste of it.

"Not gonna happen, buddy boy," I say, "Trust me, this isn't your night. I have a few tricks up my sleeve. Prepare to be carried out in second place, if you're lucky. Ha. Ha."

My inner snark shines.

"No way. You're up against the next Rick Riordan." Malik replies and runs his hands over his always perfect curls. Luke loaned me his gel, which I slather on to keep my hair pasted down, so I won't be pushing it off my forehead all night, which would disrupt my composure.

On our way to the log cabin, it starts to mist, and soon the raindrops grow larger.

Malik stops, looks back toward our cabin, and then to the log cabin. He says, "I didn't bring my bag, and it's too late to go back. Can you put my papers in your backpack so they don't get wet?"

"Sure." I unzip the front section, and there's the note Olive gave me the day I left for Lakeside right on top. She wrote Olive & Rocky in long columns and drew a big red heart with our initials in the center. I forgot it was there. It would be bad for me if it got mixed up with Malik's papers, so I stuff the note into my shorts pocket. If that paper fell into the wrong hands, I could be the butt of some serious teasing.

By the time we get inside, it's pouring. The dining hall looks completely different with benches in theater-style rows and a podium at the front. Even three layers of deodorant can't stop the sogginess swamping my armpits, but there's not one molecule of sweat on Malik. Wish I could copy him in coolness too.

On our way to our seats, I toss Olive's love note into the waste basket. I hope she doesn't kill me for that. The room fills, and Yosh and Luke sit behind us for moral support. The big night for the artists is tomorrow.

Althea taps the mike a few times before she begins. Meanwhile, Ted pushes into our row and sits on the other side of me. He and I don't exchange any words, and I set my backpack on the floor between us to block Ted from invading my space.

Althea describes the evening's format and announces, "Our first reader will be Rocky Casson."

Holy smokes! First! That is a good thing/bad thing. At least, my nerves will soon be able to recover, but going first often gets the most attention because people haven't yet slipped into a boredom coma.

I position my papers on the podium and pretend to glue my feet to the floor. This is Ms. Rotterdam's technique for readings to prevent shifting from one foot to the other as if you have to pee. That's not a good look. Now all I have to worry about is keeping my voice from changing octaves.

My presentation is flawless. I don't stumble on a single word, and I don't lose my place. When I return to my seat, Malik shakes my hand, and Ted whispers, "Wonderful. You've got this. I love that story."

Isabelle goes next, and then the others. Althea saves Malik for last, which might mean she has already decided he has the best story. Malik asks me for his papers that are in my backpack.

I wish him good luck because I'd be a piece of garbage not to do that, although I doubt he needs it. He's so in control all the time. I bet it won't rattle him to be up front and being judged.

His story is about a young water carrier who can save the world from destruction and defeat the evil archduke if he proves himself righteous and clever. The room falls silent in an eerie trance as his words captivate everyone.

Then, suddenly, he stops speaking. The calmness and confidence in his face are replaced by a gaping mouth and bewildered eyes. He shuffles his papers and stares at me as if his eyes are lasers and he's taking aim to riddle my body with bullets.

"Uh...the end," he says and leaves the podium.

"What happened up there?" I ask him when he sits down.

"You did this to me on purpose like when you messed with our clothes, but this isn't funny. This is beyond serious, man. I'm reporting you."

"What do you think I did?"

"You stole some pages of my story, and I couldn't continue."

"What? I did NOT."

"What a scummy thing to do. They were in your backpack. I trusted you."

"I didn't take them." I turn to my backpack still on the floor between me and Ted.

Ted! Oh no! Not him again. He must've taken the papers while I was at the podium. What a terrible thing to do, even to my rival. He probably thinks this is how he will get brownie points from Mom and fast track the wedding.

Malik's eyes lose their gleam and narrow. His angry voice is a whisper-shout full of accusation. "Yeah, that's what you always say. Who me? Mr. Innocent. You'll be thrown out of Lakeside. How could you be jealous enough to want to destroy me?"

The sweat, which had been running down my body, has

frozen into icy rivers. I didn't do what he says I did, but it looks bad. Heck, even I might blame me if I didn't know better.

Althea closes the program with some brief remarks that I don't listen to. As soon as she speaks her last word, she rushes to Ms. Simmons, the director, and Malik darts over to join them. They have an animated convo, and Ms. Simmons waves her hands around, looking upset and all the while keeping an eye in my direction.

I'm in trouble. My only thought is to get out of there fast so I can figure out my next move. Ted messed with the papers, but I need proof.

"Is Malik okay?" Ted asks, pretending he has no clue what just happened.

"He didn't have all his pages up there and had a panic attack. Where are his papers?" I demand.

"How would I know?" Ted asks, pretending to be innocent.

"They were right there in my backpack." I say, pointing to the floor.

"I didn't know they were there," Ted claims. He protests the same way I did that I wasn't the one who messed with the guys' clothes. This is a disaster and once again, I visualize my life circling a drain, about to disappear before I can stop it.

I turn around and say, "Hey, Yosh, Ted's driving to Milton tonight, and I'm grabbing a ride with him to check in on my grandfather. I'll go to the cabin first to get some things. See you tomorrow."

"Hey, not so fast," Yosh says. "I saw you toss Malik's paper into the trash on your way in tonight."

"No, I didn't do that," I say.

Yosh's eyes squint and his eyebrows join in the center in disbelief, but I can't tell him what was on that paper.

On my way to the door, I stop at the waste basket and grab the crumpled paper I tossed in there before someone finds it.

Luke and Yosh make their way to Ms. Simmons to give their evidence against me.

Move, Rocky, now! Luckily it stopped raining, and I charge to the grove with a head full of mush trying to make sense out of what just happened. I cast my eyes upward to the heavens and pray one of those stars will shine brighter than the others, and it will be Dad looking down on me because if he's not here, I'm totally alone.

"Dad, I need you. What should I do?" I don't bother to keep my words inside my head. No answer. During the first few months after Dad died, I often heard his voice, offering advice and even cracking jokes. But as time passes, it's harder to remember how he sounded.

Once I reach the grove, my eyes are cloudy. I blink to remove the blurriness that the tears have caused, but I don't stop. Instead, I head deeper into the woods. I want to run far, far away like Forrest Gump.

My life is ruined, and I did nothing.

PART 3:

IN THE WILDERNESS

CHAPTER 13

The well-worn path ends, and the walking becomes more treacherous as roots and underbrush cover the ground, waiting to trip me up. A low-hanging tree limb wallops me in the face. My hand reaches up to touch the spot above my eyes, and a bit of warm, sticky liquid glides down my forehead. I don't care. Why would Ted steal Malik's papers? Is he dumb enough to believe I'd be so grateful that I would give him the green light for the wedding? Mom would kick him to the curb if she caught him cheating. He obviously doesn't know her very well.

I'm lost in my thoughts until a loud rustling noise from behind scares the pants off me. Something is pursuing me and closing in fast. Panic rises from my gut. I'm defenseless out here. I think about turning back, but if I do, I'll run smack into whatever's chasing me.

Wild animals roam the woods at night. Even a kindergarten kid reads stories about wolves stalking people. Now I'm trapped here and in perfect position to be the victim for some animal's next meal.

All I can do is run. The forest becomes thicker, which prevents any starlight reaching the ground. I reach into my pocket for the all-purpose penknife with a tiny flashlight that

Ted gave me on my first day here. It's actually way cool, and I carry it with me all the time, but I didn't tell him that.

I'm about to turn on the light until I realize that would alert my pursuer to my exact location. So, I continue on in the darkness, zigzagging right and left, uphill and down, while praying hard these maneuvers will shake off whatever is following me.

The snapping twigs and loud breathing behind me intensify, and a block of fear replaces my beating heart. My oxygen tank is running on empty. I stop and crouch low near some bushes to refill my lungs. While I'm down there, I remember my fifth-grade science report about how big cats hunt by scent. I scrape at the earth to dig up clumps of dirt to smear on my face and neck to mask my smell.

Then I do something so dumb and not worthy of a teenager. Like a little kid playing hide-and-seek, I close my eyes, so if I can't see whatever is out there, it can't see me. Childish, for sure.

"Stop!" A voice shouts, echoing through the air.

It's not a wild animal chasing me. It's human. That brings on a very brief wave of relief until I realize that even if my pursuer is human, it doesn't mean I'm safe. He could be an escaped convict or an axe murderer, so I take off again, even faster, not wanting to wait to find out who's following me.

The voice shouts again, but this time it calls out my name. "Rocky!"

Hallelujah. I almost collapse. The stalker must be someone from the program. I turn toward the sound's direction, but no one is there.

"Who's there?" I yell. "Come out." I shine my light around.

"It's me." And Malik emerges from behind a tree.

"Malik! You scared me to death," I exclaim, shocked to learn that the beast chasing me is him. My hand moves to my chest to tamp down the rapid beats before they reach heart attack territory.

I direct my penlight to his face. He's leaning against a tree, whistling his words as he also catches his breath. "Give. Me. A. Minute."

"Why are you following me? Do you think I have your missing papers in my pocket?"

"I had to stop you from escaping. You have to pay for what you did. Guilty people always run."

"I didn't leave because I was guilty. I needed time alone to figure out how to handle this mess. I don't want you here with me. Go back."

"I'm not going without you."

"What is this? A citizen's arrest? I'm not going with you. Bye, bye." I wave at him and turn to go.

"You can't leave me," he begs.

"Yes, I can."

"Even if I was willing to go back, I have no idea where we are, and it's so dark."

He's right about that. While I ran, I didn't focus on where I was going. If we separate, it could be dangerous. Malik is def not the outdoorsy type, and I doubt he can handle himself in the woods. I, on the other hand, am a veteran out here thanks to many camping trips with Dad and my uncle.

I guess it's up to me to look out for him. "We might be lost, Malik. The only thing we can do is to wait until daybreak, find the lake, and follow the shoreline back to the Lakeside docks."

"It's scary out here," Malik says, shyly as if he's embarrassed to admit that.

Who's the big man now, Malik the Marvelous? But I don't rub it in. I don't want to give him another reason to hate me.

"Let's find a spot to rest until the first sign of light. Out here you don't have your mother to look out for you. You have to take care of yourself."

"You think you're so smart. You don't know everything. I don't need my mother; she needs me. If she doesn't hover and wait on me, she'd fall apart."

"Are you joking?"

"I am not," he says all serious. "She never lets me forget I'm her baby. Hey, this isn't about me. I don't have to explain anything to you. What sort of person does what you did? Is winning the prize so important that you would ruin my reading because I'm a better writer than you are?"

"I DIDN'T DO IT!" I shout, and my voice cracks into a child's squeal. I shine the penlight on my face to show him I mean every word. Malik jumps backward and his mouth forms a giant O, big enough to shove in a triple-decker Mac. It's like he's seen a real-life Dementor.

"What happened to your face?" Malik says.

Then I realize why he reacted like that. I'm covered in dirt. "Oh, yeah. I forgot about what I must look like. Pretty scary, I guess. I tried to mask my scent from the wild beast running after me who turned out to be you."

"And there's blood on your forehead. You're a mess."

"Battle scars."

"Not funny, Rocky. Where are my papers?"

"I'm not sure. I have a theory, and you will think I'm nuts, but my backpack was next to Ted. He might've taken the papers when I was reading my story."

"Ted? Why the heck would he mess me up? That makes no sense."

"It's complicated. He isn't exactly my mom's friend like I said. He and my mom want to get married."

"So?"

"So, since he's been hanging around, a lot of nasty stuff has happened to me. My theory is he took your papers to help me win, so I don't blow up the wedding plans. And for your information, Ted might be responsible for the clothes prank and pinned it on me just like he's doing now. He's involved in too many suspicious events."

"Still makes no sense," Malik says.

"I have to smoke him out and get him to admit what he's done."

"Yosh said you threw something out in the trash just before the readings and then you retrieved it when you ran out. Were those my pages?"

"No. It was something personal," I explain. "Believe me. It was not your story."

"Prove it. Show me the paper from the trash."

I reach into my pocket. It's not there. I try the other pockets. Still nothing. Olive's love note must've fallen out when I reached for the penlight. This complicates everything. That piece of paper could've helped prove my innocence. Too late now. *What a big fat stupid D.U.M.B.J.E.R.K. you are, Rocky.*

"I can't show it to you. I threw it away by mistake," I say.

"Right. You just managed to take it with you and then get rid of it. Convenient and guilty, I would say."

"It's the truth. Besides, Ted must have snatched your papers. I know this looks bad for me, but I'm sure this is another of Ted's evil deeds. I have to figure out a way to expose him. Let's find a spot to rest for the night." I shine the light around, deciding which way to go, and start walking. Malik follows me.

"Malik, do you think anyone from Lakeside will notice you're missing tonight? I covered my tracks by telling Luke and Yosh I was going home for the night with Ted, so no one would come after me." I look at him. "But you managed to follow me so a lot of good that did me."

"I told Jono I was going back to the cabin to talk to you. It'll be a while before someone misses us."

"Good. One less thing to worry about." I lead the way and pick up the pace. The ground slopes and gets steep.

A horrible howl echoes through the woods. I stop and turn. The awful noise is coming from Malik.

CHAPTER 20

I wave the penlight around, but there's no sign of Malik.

"Yow!" he screams again.

"Where are you? You better not be playing with me."

"I. Can't. Get. Up." I follow his voice and point the light on the ground. His handsome face is crunched into one giant pain ball, and his eyelids are pressed together. He's clutching his leg. I move in closer and observe gobs of blood around a branch that is sticking straight out of his lower leg as if someone shot him with an arrow. I gag on my saliva as I inspect the wound and sense a hurl coming on. I heave, but nothing disgusting comes up because my stomach is too empty.

"What happened?" I ask. One minute we're talking, and the next he's a casualty.

"I tripped and landed on a spike or something."

"I can see that."

Then he peppers me with questions as if I'm some sort of medical expert. "What is it? Is it really bad? What if I can't walk? How will I get back? Will I die out here?"

"You are not dying. Calm down. It could be better, but I'll get you back to Lakeside. I promise." I hope I'm not lying about the seriousness of his injury, but I'm also scared. I pull out the little knife attached to the penlight, and Malik goes ballistic when he sees that.

"Hey. What are you going to do? Don't cut me!"

OMG! He thinks I'm gonna operate on him. Fool. I'm no surgeon, and I'd never attempt to pull that sucker out, because it might cause a gusher.

"No one's cutting you, doofus." I remove my hoodie and my button-down shirt, and whip off my T-shirt with a sigh that I'm about to sacrifice the one with the Rubik's Cube, an all-time fave. I slice strips of cloth, which I tie together, pulling tight on the knots and then wrap it around his leg above the wound to stop the bleeding. My camping trips with Dad weren't all fooling around. He taught me first aid and some survival techniques. I'm amazed at how much I still remember.

"Am I losing a lot of blood?" Malik asks. His voice is hoarse, either from shouting or from tears that are lodged in his throat. Right after Dad died, I spent a lot of time sucking back tears because I was determined to keep them private. Sometimes when I did that, I couldn't speak.

I shine the light on his leg again. This all-purpose knife and flashlight has turned out to be pretty spectacular. Already I see that my shirt is stained bright red, but the bleeding has slowed.

"That helped," I reassure him. Malik brags about his writing, but in this situation, I'm the one with all the smarts. He'd be useless if we were in the reversed position. I bet he's never even been camping with his dad.

His eyes close again, which might not be a good sign. I can't tell if he's resting or borderline passing out so I poke him. When he doesn't respond, I do it again ten times harder, almost drilling my finger through his skin.

"Ow," he yelps.

"I'm going for help as soon it's light."

"No. You can't leave me. What if a bear comes—or a snake?"

"Chill, Malik. Nothing will happen in daylight. You can trust me. I'm a pro in the wilderness. Been camping a thousand times."

"I've never been. I'm city people. My dad is only interested in games that involve a ball."

"Well, at least you've got a dad," I snarl, then quickly regret my harsh tone. It's the pressure building up inside me. I know kids have dads, and it isn't anyone's fault my dad died and theirs didn't.

"Sorry." His mouth droops like a sad-faced bulldog when he says that.

"Forget it. It's just I'm on edge because my mom is threatening to send my life into a tailspin with another major change. At least you've got two big brothers to complain to. I don't even have sibs."

"Half brothers. Same dad, different moms."

"Is that why you don't get along with them? Did they beat you up when you were little?"

"No hitting. Not allowed in my house. Mostly they ignore me because I don't play sports, and they're fantastic athletes. My dad doesn't care about writing or good grades."

"I didn't know there were parents on this planet who don't care about grades. Even though I'm into soccer like my dad, who almost went pro, he always insisted on schoolwork first."

It's fascinating that Malik, who lives on easy street with plenty of money and is at the top of his class and never has to do anything around the house, doesn't have a perfect life.

"I guess your family is complicated," I say.

"Isn't everyone's?"

"Mine certainly is. I've got a friend, Max, who has to cope with a new baby brother. And what about Luke and Yosh who always have to explain how they can be brothers? That must be frustrating."

"My leg is getting numb. Is that a bad sign?" Malik seems to think I'm his doctor just because I can make a tourniquet.

I know what he wants to hear, so I oblige. "It's good. Means it won't hurt so much anymore." I hope there's an ounce of truth in my answer because otherwise the branch has done serious damage.

"How about trying to stand? I'll help you." I'm eager for him to test his leg.

"Okay," he replies in a shaky voice, definitely not confident about this experiment.

"Put your arm over my shoulder." We struggle, but I succeed in hoisting him upright, which lasts for all of a second before he crumbles to the ground.

"You're in no condition to walk. We'll stay here until daybreak."

"I can't understand how your mom would agree to marry someone you think is evil."

"Mind control. He has erased her smart cells. I have a list of everything he has done to me, and I'm writing a tell-all story about him."

"Maybe this is all your fantasy on steroids. Family change is rough. Just ask my brothers who had to suffer with a beautiful, talented, brilliant new baby brother who grew up hating to play football. You make it seem like this Ted guy is an evil wizard. Maybe your creative juices are gearing up to write a blockbuster fantasy." Malik snickers, which means either he is better or his leg has lost all feeling. That would be real bad.

"I'm not writing any fantasies," I say.

"Yeah, family stuff sucks sometimes."

CHAPTER 21

A sliver of daylight peeks through the trees and wakes me, although I can't even remember falling asleep. The moisture in the air from overnight dew smells like clean laundry. If I could, I'd sleep longer, but I don't have that luxury. Malik could get an infection, then this accident would turn more serious, and I'd be the person responsible. Malik might start a list about my evil deeds as if I am his personal Doctor Doom.

Malik stirs too.

"How's the leg?" I ask.

"Still numb. No sensation below the knee, but I've got to pee or I'll die. Can you help me hop over to a tree?"

"Sure." This is beyond awkward, but there's no choice, and I have to hurry because my bladder alerted me that it is ready to overflow.

"Sling your arm over my shoulders. Don't put any weight on that leg and pay attention to where you're going," I instruct him.

Malik pulls himself up, using me as a post to steady himself. He takes three hops to a nearby tree and leans on the trunk with one hand. I leave him there and scoot away to do my business.

"Are you finished?" I ask when I'm done, not wanting to go near him and interrupt anything.

When Malik says, "All set. Help me hop back," I move in, and we reverse our earlier effort. I lower him near a large tree as if he's breakable. Bending his leg might cause the pain to rage again. Malik moans when his butt hits the ground.

"I...could...come...with...you," he says, his voice hesitant and maybe on the verge of crying.

"Dude, you're in no shape to trek through the woods. I have to go alone. Plus, you wouldn't be in this mess if it wasn't for me, so it's all on me to fix this."

"Having a stick of wood in my leg isn't your fault unless you put it there. Did you?" he says, and quickly adds, "Only kidding. Or maybe not."

Unbelievable. I am not the villain, despite what has happened. "Malik, before I go, I need your T-shirt."

He gulps, suspecting I'm about to do something horrible to him. He doesn't trust my strange request, but I guess I wouldn't either if I were him.

"Why?" he asks, eyes blinking like he's sending coded messages for help.

"Don't get worked up. I'm gonna make a signal flag that you can wave if someone comes near. Otherwise no one will spot you here sitting on the ground."

He removes his shirt while I go off in search of long thin stick. There's so much forest debris, it's easy to find the perfect broken branch. I tie his shirt to the top of it and hand the stick to him. He holds it, and I snap my feet together and salute this make-shift flag like I'm a regular stand-up comedian.

"Let me check your boo-boo before I leave," I joke, trying to make his injury seem less serious than it is. The bleeding has stopped. The color of dark brown dried blood blends in with his skin more than it would on mine. When doctors remove the branch, his leg might spout like a geyser again. In any case, it'll hurt like heck to yank that sucker out. I hope they give him anesthesia. Better to be fast asleep. If not, his mom will hear his screams back home in New York.

"No more bleeding," I say, but don't share with him all my worries about infection and what might lie ahead for him.

"Aren't you afraid you'll get lost?" Malik asks.

"I'm heading downhill toward the lake. From there, I'll hug the shoreline and find help. My dad taught me a trick that hikers use so they won't walk in circles in the woods. You imagine a string connecting two points straight in front of you and follow that pretend string to keep you walking in a straight line. No prob, buddy; everything is under control."

"You wouldn't leave me here so you can collect the prize and fly off to L.A., would you?"

Even now he still suspects me. "Bro, you've got the wrong idea about me."

"I was mainly joking, except for my scared side, which wasn't."

I have to prove myself to Malik, and when I come back with help, he'll understand I've always been a stand-up guy.

"Rocky..." Malik's voice drops off.

"You'll be okay, dude." I give him a gentle punch on the shoulder like I would do to my best bud Max. Then I reassure him, "Maniacs stay hidden until dark. You're safe now. Relax."

That's a lie, but a good one considering the circumstances. I leave and use the penknife to make small cuts around the height of my shoulders on the trees like leaving bread crumbs so I can find my way back. I have to clear my name like a person who is desperate for DNA tests to get his prison sentence canceled. And I'll need a brilliant lawyer from the Innocence Project to come to my rescue.

For now, it's Rocky, the criminal; Rocky, the cheater; Rocky, the sabotager.

If I stay focused on my mission and help Malik, maybe I can reclaim my reputation.

CHAPTER 22

My outdoor skills pay off when I spot the calm blue-green water in the distance. I applaud my success, and in no time, I'm at the lake, pulling off my kicks and socks. I jump in to wash off my bruised forehead and yesterday's dirt so I don't scare people when I ask them for help. Malik had a shocked reaction when he saw my hide-my-scent face yesterday.

I cup my hands to drink which makes me feel more human. I put my Nikes back on and stuff my socks into a pocket because wearing squishy-wet socks is icky.

Ready to continue, I look both ways as if I'm about to cross a busy street and face the fact that I have no clue which way to go. All the running through the woods has turned me around. Lakeside could be to the right or the left. For no good reason, I choose to go right.

I walk along the edge of the lake and only stray when fallen tree trunks and other obstacles block me. Sometimes I have to climb over low branches or scoot under bushes that are in my way, but I always return to the shoreline.

The lake is wide and juts in and out, so you can't see much beyond the bend, and it makes the distance around longer. I'm about to give up on this direction and do a U-turn when I see a light through the pines. I start sprinting toward a small house with a burst of renewed energy.

I get closer and eyeball a dumpy cabin with peeling paint, cracked windows and rusty barrels in the yard. The place was probably white once, but there are only a few remaining clean spots. This cabin must have been on the losing end of a major mud fight. Next to it, there's a small dock with a tired-looking boat tied up.

I crouch low and position myself under a window to do surveillance. The room seems large enough for one person—no family lives here. The table is tiny with only a single chair. A twin bed is along one wall, and it has a very rough looking blanket. It's odd that the bed has no pillow, but I guess whoever lives here wants it to be as uncomfortable as possible.

While I'm scoping out the room, an old man comes from somewhere in the back. He sits in a dark brown chair with stuffing spurting out all over. I duck so he won't catch me spying on him. I count to ten before I lift my head inch by inch until it seems safe to look in. The man has a gray beard bushy enough to make a good nest for a small animal, and his hair looks like he has been recently electrocuted.

A silver-handled knife hangs from his belt, which holds up his raggedy, patched pants. I spot two rifles on the wall. The weapons should be my signal to run, but who knows when I'll find another cabin, and Malik is in tough shape. Fingers crossed this guy only uses the rifles for hunting, and I don't mean people.

Good thing Mom isn't here to witness this. She'd bust a blood vessel if she knew I plan to ask a stranger who owns rifles for help. This is against all the rules she has tattooed on my brain since I was a baby, but I have no choice. Dad used to say, "Life happens, and when you find yourself in a tough situation, you just have to man up."

I tighten all my muscles to man up and promise that if I survive this, I will not make Mom worry about me again. EVER. She'd be way sad if something bad happened to me.

I knock on the door two times, and a few seconds later, I come face-to-face with a strange and grisly old man.

CHAPTER 23

The man peers around the door which is half-opened so he's ready to slam it shut in a second.

"Who do we have here?" he asks. "A caller so early. Are you lost, boy?" His voice is hoarse because he probably hasn't used it in forever.

When he speaks, I notice open spaces where teeth should be, and the teeth he does have are a disgusting, dark yellowish brown. I bet he doesn't own any mouthwash. But I'm for sure not getting close enough to find out.

I begin to tell him about Malik when a mangy dog that is as high as my waist bounds forward, forcing me to step back. I almost lose my balance, but I catch myself before I fall. The dog's black eyes are fixed on me, and his tail stands at attention.

"He ain't gonna eat you, boy," the man sneers. "He just finished breakfast; he's full for a while."

Un-freaking-believable. Who jokes about dogs eating people? Gross. The dog looks like a biter, too, and I have no confidence his owner would lift a finger to hold him back if he goes on the attack.

This should be my cue to flee while I still can, but for Malik's sake, I shouldn't run. I have to stand my ground. Maybe it isn't right to judge this man by his appearance. Dad used to tell me you don't know if a book is any good only by its cover. I guess I forgot Dad's lesson when I put Ted's beard and eyebrows on my list as strikes against him. I'll have to cross those items off when I get back. They aren't worthy criticisms.

Trembling, while keeping an eagle-eye on the vicious dog, I begin with the words, "Malik, he's my friend," and I'm surprised I refer to him as my friend. I'm not sure he'd agree with that description of our relationship, but he's not here to object.

I continue, "He hurt himself bad. He fell on a branch, and it's stuck in his leg. He's in a lot of pain and can't walk. We attend a summer program at the Lakeside cabins. It must not be too far from here. Can you call them? Does 911 respond here? Is there a doctor nearby? Is it possible you can drive us to the hospital?"

I reach deep into my lungs for more air and sputter, "I need help."

"Slow down. That's a mess of words you flung at me. What were you and your friend doing in the woods at night by yourselves? Was this a camping adventure gone haywire, or were you two up to no good?" He laughs, but I don't understand what's so humorous.

"If you call Lakeside, I'm sure they'll come to get us. Their cabins are also on this lake," pleading for help.

"This area is enormous. My cabin is in the tail end of the lake, and there's nothing near here. I never heard of a place called Lakeside, but I guess it wasn't someone too clever who thought that name up. I mind my own business, and I don't have a car or a phone. Don't need them."

No phone? Seriously? He's living in the Dark Ages. This isn't just old-fashioned; it's strange. I ask, "Then can you come with me and help me get Malik to a doctor?"

He eyes me up and down which gives me the willies. "I

don't get involved in other people's problems. Find someone else to bother. You picked the wrong place."

He closes the door, but I push against it and raise my voice. "What? No! I'm not going anywhere. I found you, so you have to help me. Please."

This man must be completely ignorant about the unwritten rule that grownups are supposed to come to a kid's rescue.

"I don't gotta do anything. You were old enough to find your way here, find your way to somewhere else."

I crank up my arguing skills and play the kid card to soften his hard heart. "This is the first cabin I saw. What if I get lost? I'm only thirteen."

"Demanding, aren't you? I leave people alone, and they leave me alone. It's the truce I made with society long ago."

The dog glares at me but doesn't move. If I don't get help for Malik soon, who knows what might happen to him? I don't have the luxury to hope I can find a nicer person, so I stand straighter and pretend like Dad is beside me, pumping me with courage.

"Sir," I say with a voice full of fake bravery to convince myself I'm not petrified. "I'm sorry you don't want to be around people, and you don't have to like me, but Malik needs help. Now!"

He gawks at me. Boy, did I ever pick the wrong place. My rudeness dam bursts from fear and anger, and the next words that tumble from my mouth astonish me. "I bet whatever happened to you was all your fault. I'm leaving."

Whoa, tough guy, I think as I'm about to run. I pray he's too slow to catch me.

"Stop." The old man holds up his hand like a traffic cop. "You're a stubborn fellow, aren't you? But, you might get lost, and that would be on my conscience, too."

Too? He must be lugging around gallons of guilt. Maybe it's best I don't know what he did.

"Thank you very much, Mister...? Mister...?" He doesn't give me his name, so I continue without it. "I'm sorry I got so upset." I force myself to smile, hoping he'll accept my apology.

He doesn't smile back, but his voice isn't as hostile as it was. "We'll bring your friend back here and take the boat to your camp so he won't have to be walking too much."

"One more tiny thing," I whisper in a scaredy-cat's little voice, afraid I might set this guy off and cause his mood to shift back to being mean again. "Could I get some water and food for him? You have water, don't you?"

"Water? Of course I have water. Can't live without water. I'm sure they taught you that in school. I dug a well. Come to the kitchen, but you'd better not be fussy."

I'm hesitant to go back there with him where he could trap me and close off any chance of escape. Mom drilled the stranger danger rules into me since I was little, and this is one of the biggies. I swallow hard, stand as tall as I can and follow him to the kitchen. It's a tight squeeze in there for the two of us, so I try to shrink my body and not bump into him.

He opens the fridge. "How about a piece of this? I can cut some off for your friend," he asks, holding up a plate with either a dead squirrel or a stretched-out rat. Nausea flows up into my mouth.

"Um...no...can I bring a bottle of water and maybe some cookies?"

"I don't have a bottle." He grabs a jar off a shelf with a metal cover dotted with spots of orange rust and hands it to me. I open it, and detect an unusual smell, but I can't place it. I have no idea what's been in there, but I bet it wasn't anything delicious. Still, it looks clean enough. It'll have to do. I fill it and tighten the lid.

He opens a cupboard, and the bottom shelf overflows with beef jerky as if he bought out the entire store. He takes out two sticks of that and a box of crackers and stuffs everything into a small bag, including the jar of water.

"And my name is Rocky," I say, expecting him to respond with his name, but he doesn't.

"Let's go," he says. As he gets to the door, he removes one of the rifles from the wall and puts bullets in it.

ALARM! ALARM! DANGER! DANGER!

The words scream inside my head as if my brain is a smoke detector warning me to evacuate.

CHAPTER 24

"Rifle? Why do you need a rifle?" I ask, drifting toward the door, ready to push him and run for my life.

"Listen, boy, you don't have to be scared, but you've got to be prepared in the woods. Would you argue with a bear like you did with me and persuade him not to make you his lunch? Ignore the rifle."

He has a point, but still, guns are dangerous. I've had enough lockdown drills at school to know that. "You can be certain I won't touch it."

As we walk, I pace myself to keep it manageable for the old dude. The sun is higher now, and I hope the guy doesn't stroke out in this heat. I remove my hoodie and tie it around my waist.

I expect finding my way back will be easy because I'm following the cuts I made on the trees. When we're close, I call out, "Malik! Malik!"

No response.

I shout again, and my voice cracks as if I snapped a vocal cord. Nothing. Panic rolls through my body. What if I never find him? He'll assume I abandoned him and never had any intention of returning with help. And this man might bust a gut if he thinks I dragged him out here on a wild goose chase.

Not sure what I should do if I can't find Malik soon. I stop and look slowly in each direction. Finally, I catch a glimpse of the T-shirt flag. Yipee! *Good work, Rocky*. Making that thing was a masterful stroke. I congratulate myself and race ahead. Malik is sleeping on the ground. At least, I hope he's sleeping. I nudge him and say his name again. He startles, and I grin in relief. The white parts of his eyeballs are reddish. This kid has been doing some serious crying. I always wanted to keep my tears private after Dad died, so I'm not gonna mention that I noticed that.

"I brought help," I tell him.

The old man moves closer to Malik, and I worry Malik will hyperventilate when he gets a load of this guy with that mess of hair on his head and face.

I tug on Malik's upper body so he can sit up.

"Malik, is it?" the man says. "You sure got yourself hurt, didn't you? Next time, watch where you're going. Okay, kid, come help me lift up your friend."

"Thanks for coming," Malik says to the old guy.

"Can I give him some water first?" I ask.

"Okay," the man replies.

Malik's nostrils crunch up as he gets close to the jar as if he's trying to hold his breath and drink at the same time, which isn't possible. He gives up and sips almost half the water. Sometimes when life hands you a smelly jar, you have to drink so you won't die. I offer him crackers, but he refuses them.

The old man says, "Eating can wait. Time to move along. Put your arm around him and hook it under his armpit, and I'll do the same on the other side."

I do as I'm told.

"Okay, up," the man commands, and together we pull on Malik.

Then he turns toward Malik and says, "Sling your arms over our shoulders, but give me more of your weight. Your puny little friend probably will cave from holding you." Boy, the guy will probably faint when he sees how strong I am. He has underestimated me. Malik follows his instructions.

The three of us walk side by side until the path narrows, and we're forced to adjust into more of a long line than a wide one. The going is tricky, but the old guy has a good grip on Malik who is hop-stepping the whole way. Must be exhausting.

When the man's cabin appears, Malik, who is used to high-class stuff, doesn't react to the dilapidated place. I bet if he were present in the moment, he'd have a few thorny zingers to describe this junk heap.

We head straight for the little dock. The man half carries Malik and deposits him on the back seat and points to a little triangle piece of wood in the boat's front, saying, "Kid, you sit there."

Boy, lucky I have a small butt or this seat would be a problem. The boat is as grungy as the cabin and smells like dead fish. At least, I hope that's the odor and not dead people. I read that dead bodies stink the worst. Puke City.

The man climbs onto the middle bench, unties the boat and pushes off from the dock. He stows his rifle under the seat, lifts the oars, and places them in their metal holders.

"Ready, Malik?" he says.

"Ready," Malik answers. He isn't talking much. He must hurt pretty bad.

The man says, "I'll stay close to the shoreline" He turns to look at me. "You keep your eyes open for your camp." He rows and huffs, out of breath already, which worries me.

"Okay, and thank you again for helping."

"Time for the truth about why you two were in the woods by yourselves at night with no supplies and no adult."

I guess I owe him an explanation after all he's doing for us. "Lakeside is a program for high school kids doing creative writing, and this kid,"—I point at Malik—"is an awesome author. Anyway, when he had to read his story in front of everyone, some pages were missing, and he blamed me for taking them to screw him out of winning the big prize."

"Because he thinks you're jealous of him?" the man asks.

"Maybe I am," I admit, "but I swear I didn't take them. But the evidence points only to me. I ran so I could figure out how to clear my name. I wasn't planning to stay away for long, but then there was a strange noise behind me, and I ran deeper into the woods. Turns out the noise was Malik following me, but by then the two of us were lost, and it was dark. He fell and landed on the sharp end of a branch. That's the truth." I cross my heart. "When we get to Lakeside, I'm gonna be in the worst trouble of my life."

He pulls on the oars in even strokes, and we glide on the water. "So, they believe you stole the papers and then panicked. You sure did act guilty."

"But how could I convince everyone I didn't do it?"

"You should have stayed to defend yourself. How are you going to explain your running to your dad or mom?"

"Um...no...that couldn't happen."

"Why not?"

"I don't have an actual father anymore. He died a while back."

"Sorry, sonny. Too bad. Listen, you've got to stay and fight. You may have a boxer's name, Rocky, but you don't want to be the kind of fighter who spends the whole bout hanging on the ropes so the other guy doesn't hit him. That isn't a winning strategy."

This guy knows his prizefighting. He continues, "I became a hermit because I ran from something years ago, and I also did nothing wrong. I should have stayed, but like you, I was sure no one would believe my story."

Wow, I bet this guy was accused of something a lot worse than stealing part of a short story. I'm afraid to ask what he did because he seems volatile, but if he didn't want me to know, why would he mention it? My internal debate gives me a headache, so I rev up my courage and ask, "What happened?"

"I'll tell you because I'm sorry about what you've got going on, but you must promise never to tell a living soul. I don't want anyone coming around here to talk to me because you couldn't keep your mouth shut. I want to be left alone."

"Promise."

"Years ago, I was at the county fair with my little sister, who was ten. I was almost twenty. She was beautiful with long, brown pigtails, a big old dimple and a few freckles under her eyes which always blossomed in the summer. Everyone, including me, loved her, but people didn't love me."

He for sure isn't the loveable type, and not too likeable either.

He continues, "There were times I wished so much people loved me like they did her. Jealousy can be like a slithering snake coiling around you as it squeezes the life out of you. Anyway, my sister insisted I take her on the Ferris wheel. She was a feisty kid, a daredevil type who never listened to anyone. The Ferris wheel stopped when we were at the top to pick up passengers, and Susie jiggled the car until it rocked wildly. I yelled at her to stop, but she wouldn't. Then she stood up, telling me she was trying to touch the sky. As she reached up, I moved to grab her and sit her back down, but I was too late. She tumbled out and died."

What a horrible story. I know I should say something nice to him, but I'm not sure what.

Finally I say, "I'm sorry your sister died." That lame line makes me regret all those times I was super critical about people saying dumb stuff to me after Dad died. I guess it's tougher than I thought to find the right words in sad situations.

"Her death devastated my parents," the man continues, "and they blamed me, but it wasn't my fault. The day after her funeral, I left town and never returned. I did odd jobs for years and then settled here on the lake. That's how sure I was people would jump to the conclusion I pushed her. But why would I do that? She was my baby sister, and I loved her."

So he was also accused of jealousy like me. I wonder if, when I'm a hundred years old, I could wind up living in the woods, wearing torn, smelly clothes with a rifle slung over my shoulder. I might have a scruffy beard that drags on the ground and also be a hermit with no name.

PART 4:

BACK AT LAKESIDE

CHAPTER 25

Thinking about the little girl on the Ferris wheel is haunting me. I catch myself glancing down to watch the schools of tiny fish swimming carefree just below the water's surface, instead of concentrating on the shoreline like I'm supposed to. It's kinda cool how those fish stay in perpetual motion and change direction every couple of seconds as if they can't make up their minds which way to go. I understand their feeling of confusion and wish I could dive in and join them.

We move around another rather large piece of land, and finally, Lakeside's docks appear. In my excitement, I jump up, pointing and hollering, "Here! Here!" and the boat seesaws violently.

The guy yells, "Sit down, you fool! Never stand up in a boat. Are you trying to drown yourself—or us?"

His anger sears my skin. I can almost feel blisters forming. But he's right. I know you're not supposed to do that. I lost my cool for a moment. Maybe the boat's shaking reminded him of his little sister rocking the Ferris wheel.

"Hey, Malik!" I shout. "You'll be at the doctor's soon." I can't wait to have a grown-up in charge of him so I'm off the hook. Heck, I need my own problem fixer, too.

By now, I bet Ms. Simmons, my judge and jury, has already

pronounced sentence on me. How will I explain this mess to Mom when I can't understand it myself? Running away still seems like a good option, unless Ms. Simmons puts me in lock-up. Lock-up—that's a pitiful joke about all this, and it fails big time.

The nameless man rows close to the dock, lifts the oars out of the water, and ties up the boat. It's still early, so everyone's probably at breakfast. The lakefront is empty. The mere thought of food starts my stomach hollering for fresh supplies to be sent down. I haven't eaten in forever.

"Go, get help," the old man orders me.

I wish I knew his name, but I guess if you want to maintain your hermit status, you don't tell. "Thanks, Mister," I say and scramble onto the dock, taking off up the path to the office. I push open Ms. Simmons's door without knocking. She's at her desk. Her eyes bug out at the sight of me. I must look freakin' awful.

"Luke and Yosh reported you and Malik missing a short time ago right after they got up. I contacted Ted immediately if case you were with him. He persuaded me to give you a little more time. He thought you might've gone for a walk and would show up for breakfast. Where were you? Where is Malik? You have a lot of explaining to do after last night."

Boy, maybe Ted has powers to shape-shift people. He could transform me into an armadillo with a hard armor shell to withstand the verbal pounding coming my way, but knowing him, he'd turn me into a soft, squishy panda instead.

"Where is Malik?" she asks again with the force of a tidal wave barreling toward me. "I was sure he was with you."

"He was. I mean, he is with me. He's hurt. An old man brought us here in his boat. He's at the docks. Malik needs a doctor. He fell and landed on a sharp branch, which is sticking out of his leg." My words flow like a running faucet without a shut-off switch.

I open the door to head back to the waterfront and glance over my shoulder to make sure she's right behind me. She is. On the way, she calls for an ambulance and then contacts Jono on her two-way to wait at the office and bring the paramedics to the lake with a stretcher ASAP.

When we get there, we see Malik sitting on the sand, but there's no sign of the boat or its owner. She rushes to Malik's side.

"Are you okay?" she asks and then rests her eyes on the stick stuck in his leg.

"It hurts," Malik says as if she couldn't figure that out.

Ms. Simmons moves away to make a call, and I approach Malik. "Bro, you'll soon be as perfect as you always were. Too bad the old dude didn't wait around. I didn't get a chance to thank him." I guess he meant it when he said he wasn't interested in talking to people. It must be depressing to live your life alone without family or friends.

"How's your leg?" I ask.

"Same," he says. "I thanked Mr. Maxwell for both of us."

"Mr. Maxwell? He told you his name?" I'm both surprised and jealous that the old guy didn't find me worthy of knowing his name. It stinks when people don't trust you.

"Why wouldn't he tell me? I asked him," Malik says.

"Um...no reason." I must reek of dishonesty, otherwise Mr. Maxwell would've told me his name. He didn't trust me to keep his secret.

"Malik, how can I drum it into you that I was not the one who took your papers? I'm not that kind of guy."

Before he can answer, Jono arrives leading two men carrying a stretcher. The medics move as a well-trained unit to raise Malik and put him on the stretcher without jostling the branch lodged in his leg. We all head back up to the office, where they load Malik into the waiting ambulance. Without thinking, I move to get in with him until Ms. Simmons puts her hand on my shoulder and guides me toward the office.

"Jono will go with him," she says. "You're staying here. You have a lot to answer for, Rocky."

CHAPTER 26

Following Ms. Simmons's gray swishing ponytail is hypnotic. I collapse onto a chair, my knees buckling from exhaustion and starvation. I contemplate confessing to end this nightmare, so I can ask for a last meal like every other condemned man.

My stomach assumes that thought is its cue to let out a rumble louder than a crashing avalanche. It succeeds in drawing Ms. Simmons's attention. If I wasn't so hungry, I'd be super embarrassed.

She asks, "When did you last eat?"

"Dinner yesterday."

"So the man who rowed you back didn't feed you?"

"No, but we did have water."

"We'll go to breakfast and then deal with this, but you will sit at my table. Your roommates consider you persona non grata."

I don't ask what those words mean, but from her tone, I know they aren't good. I sense there's a giant letter "C" branded on my forehead for *cheater*, alerting people to keep their distance.

"Will Ted be there?"

"Ted's in the parking lot waiting for your mother."

"My mother's coming?"

"We notified her last night about the incident, and she wanted to be here to talk to you. Ted is calling her now to let her know you're back and in one piece." I wonder if Ms. Simmons wanted Mom here so I could get a ride home today when she kicks me out.

As soon as we enter the log cabin, the hubbub and clashing of utensils stops. I do the perp walk to Ms. Simmons's table and suck in gobs of air, hoping to keep my face at a cool temperature so it doesn't bloom into a giant ugly tomato.

The dining hall has never been this quiet. I wish I could miniaturize myself and dive into my glass of OJ to hide. Without that option, I keep my head down and stuff my face, hoping to fill the empty pit inside me. It takes three helpings of French toast and a load of scrambled eggs to accomplish that task.

When I'm stuffed, I say, "Ms. Simmons, can I go to my cabin first to brush my teeth and change my clothes? I'm such a mess from last night. My mother will freak if she sees me like this." I maintain an even tone so my request sounds reasonable, and I don't arouse any suspicion about my true motive.

She nods in agreement. As I get up to go, she says, "You need to be back in the office in twenty minutes in clean clothes with your teeth brushed and hair combed."

"I will." But once I'm outside, I start to run to the lake, planning to go back to the old man's cabin and beg him for asylum like a refugee at the border. He might take me in as his last chance to redeem himself. Running away may not be the smartest move, but right now that's all my brain can come up with.

This situation is way worse than after Dad died, and I screwed up for a while, taking a few too many "sick" days and missing lots of homework. Eventually, I got my act together, but this trouble is more like an earthquake combined with tornados in the middle of a Cat 5 hurricane.

I consider myself basically a good kid, maybe even a super-good kid, but how can I convince Ms. Simmons of that? Yes, Malik's papers were in my backpack, and yes, Yosh saw me throw a paper away that he assumes was Malik's. I can deny it forever, but Ms. Simmons has more than enough evidence to convict me.

I'm sure Mom will believe I'm innocent. I mean, I'm pretty sure she'll believe me.

"She might or she might not, Rocket Man. But she can't help you. Only you can solve this problem."

Olive! I spin around, and there she is. I reach out to hug her, but my arms wind up wrapping around myself. I can't grab onto her.

"You can't touch me," she says, "I'm like a hologram floating in your memory."

"Huh?"

"Weren't you contemplating running away now?" She displays a wise-guy smirk as if this is one big joke.

She's so lifelike. I answer her as if the image is the real Olive. "Yes, because you don't know what I'm going—"

"I do know what you're going through. You are, once again, in Trouble City."

"Yup."

"So, that's why your brain summoned me, Rocket Man."

Is that a thing? Could I be so desperate that my mind sees people who aren't really there? That's messed up, but then again after Dad died, his voice was often inside my head, giving me advice. It shook me up at first, but I got used to hearing him and even started to like our convos.

"Olive, tell me what to do," I say.

"I don't agree with running away. Get real."

"Mr. Maxwell also told me not to run because it broadcasts guilt."

"Who is Mr. Maxwell?" she asks. I guess she doesn't know everything that's rolling around in my head.

"An old dude I met. I'll tell you about him later. We need a plan. My entire future is at stake."

The hologram's eyebrows gather together to form a unibrow, a very furious unibrow. "No, we do not need a plan," Olive says. "*You* need a plan! You're like a turtle; untuck your head and fix this. This time I'm dissolving our partnership. We're history."

"What? Why? No! You can't abandon me." She doesn't answer, and her image walks into the lake and disintegrates into particles above the water until she vanished. I've been dumped by a hologram. I squeeze my eyes shut and pop them open real fast, hoping she'll reappear. Nope. She's gone. Without even her imaginary help, I'm double-doomed.

I reach down and pick up a smooth gray stone, lying by itself on the sand and make a wish before I skim it across the lake. When I reopen my fist, the stone has been transformed into my beating heart, pulsing in my hand. Eager to get rid of the bloody mess, I sidearm fling it, but instead of skimming the surface, it sinks into the water along with my despair.

I turn and head to my cabin, scrapping any plans of escape. There I brush my teeth and roll my tongue around to enjoy the minty freshness. I change my shirt, and I'm halfway back to the office when I remember I forgot to comb my hair. Too late now. I try to pat it into place. It is what it is.

Ms. Simmons has the power over my life. Depending on what she does, I may never play varsity soccer or get a college scholarship. I'll be the contagious kid at school destined to be shunned. The irresistible urge to run is still present, when an invisible hand on my arm gently steers me back toward the office.

CHAPTER 27

By instinct, I turn around, not really expecting to see anyone there, not even a hologram. I feel it is Dad's touch, and he's guiding me to make the right decision.

In front of the office, I spot Mom marching back and forth like a soldier in basic training. She seems full of nervous energy. Can't blame her. She rushes over and clenches me in a humongous hug.

"I was so worried," she says and starts kissing me all over my face.

"Okay, Mom. I'm okay." I move away because this greeting has officially crossed into the zone of embarrassment.

"We'll get this sorted out," she says. I wonder where she gets her confidence from considering she is missing all the deets.

"Sorry I left without telling anyone, but I didn't know what else to do," I say. "Then Malik trailed me, and things got complicated." Complicated and dangerous. This is the stuff of great books. Someday this entire episode may become part of an award-winning story with the odd and intriguing Mr. Maxwell as the main character.

When Mom reaches out to pat my cheek, Olive steps out from behind her.

"Hey, Rocky," she says. This version of her appears to be

authentic, but if I hug her and my arms wrap around myself again, I'll look like a durk in front of everyone. So instead, I lift my hand in a weak wave, afraid to commit to anything more until I have solid proof that she isn't a figment of my robust imagination.

Olive beams at me, but I'm still cautious. She says, "Your mom asked if I wanted to come to see you, and voilá, here I am." She flings her arms into the air as if she's a genie that poofed out of a lantern or something. "You have bruises on your cheeks and a doozy on your forehead."

"It's nothing," I say.

Mom introduces Olive as my best friend to Ms. Simmons, who shakes her hand. She couldn't do that unless Olive is real. My heart soars to the stratosphere and returns in a joyful journey. Not only is Olive here, but she isn't mad at me like the dopey hologram was.

I move closer to her and tap her on the shoulder to double check her realness.

"I know you're happy to see me because we've got another mess to clean up." Olive uses "we," which is reassuring. I'm no longer the dumpee.

Ms. Simmons invites all of us into her office. Ted's already inside. He smiles at me, and I nod to him. There are two chairs in the tiny space. Mom and I sit, and Olive and Ted stand behind us. Ms. Simmons takes her place at her desk and says. "Rocky, this is—"

I cut her off, which is rude and will probably be another strike against me, but I have to ask. "Sorry, can you tell me how Malik is? Did they get the stick out of his leg?"

Mom heaves out a breath, and her face goes pale. I guess no one told her what happened to him. Even when it isn't their kid who got hurt, moms' reflex worry systems start to vibrate.

Ms. Simmons says, "They have removed the, uh, branch,

cleaned out the wound, and stitched him up. They're loading him with antibiotics and giving him a tetanus shot. He should be back here soon."

"That's excellent," I say. Like Mr. Maxwell, I don't need another thing on my conscience.

Ms. Simmons picks up a piece of paper from her desk and studies it for a moment before raising her storm-cloud-looking eyes to meet mine. My butt squirms as if red ants are crawling up my crack and nibbling my skin as they go. Her face shows zero emotion, which is actually frightening.

"You are being accused of mishandling Malik's papers. That is as bad as cheating or plagiarizing. Do you understand?"

"But I didn't do it. I gave him the papers I had in my backpack." My calf muscles start to cramp. Definitely from tension.

Looking down at her desk, she says, "He was missing two pages, and you were the only one who had them. I have no choice but to write to your teacher and principal about this incident."

I wish my eyeballs were on a spring mechanism so they could reach over to read the letters she wrote, but unable to do that, my mind imagines what they might say.

One is probably to the principal of Tucker Middle.

Dear Principal Gravel, I am sorry to inform you that Ronald Owen Casson, Junior, has committed the unthink...

Then the vision changes, and the other words become unreadable because the paper catches fire and swirls into the air, turning into a gray, fragile ash as it burns.

My chest sinks into my backbone like there's no longer any heart or lungs to keep it propped up. I hear Ms. Simmons explaining that she regrets this situation we find ourselves in.

I shut my eyes for a second and imagine the second letter to Ms. Rotterdam, my constant cheerleader:

Dear Ms. Rotterdam, I have the sad duty to write about a distressing incident at Lakeside this summer with one of your students, Ronald Owen Casson, Junior. He is responsible for an unforgiv...

This letter doesn't catch fire, but the words blur as I imagine Ms. Rotterdam's tears falling in giant globs on the paper.

"Rocky, are you even paying attention?" Ms. Simmons shakes me out of my hallucinations.

"Er...yes, ma'am."

I may never be allowed to play on a team again. Without soccer, I'll lose my connection to Dad—my backyard trainer, my biggest fan, and my would-be agent planning my career and dreaming of all the possibilities ahead of me.

Ms. Simmons says. "Rocky, it isn't helpful for you to resist taking responsibility for your actions. Do you understand that?"

She keeps asking if I understand.

I understand.

I understand.

I understand I'm being accused of a crime I didn't commit.

Mom puts her hand on mine and says, "Rocky, tell everyone what you think happened to Malik's papers. I'm sure there's a simple explanation. The truth can heal. You and I had a hard lesson about honesty and secrets last year which I regret."

"But why do I need to be forgiven? I...didn't...do...it." My voice waffles, because I can't offer any other explanation about Malik's papers, except to accuse Ted and I have no proof yet. "I gave Malik the pages I had and what Yoshi saw me throw in the wastebasket wasn't part of Malik's story, it was an old letter. I swear it."

"I believe you!" Ted says with a force strong enough to crumble the office walls. He seems to have lost that old witch's cackle I hated. He puts a hand on my shoulder just like Dad always did, and I don't shrug it off.

"Rocky," he advises, "fight for your reputation. I will support you."

But can I trust him? He probably wants me to lower my guard before he walks me to the guillotine. Heck, maybe I'll be able to see my own head roll away when he slices it off. Grossitude.

I say, "No, Ted, I'll fix this myself."

Ms. Simmons says, "If the paper you put in the trash wasn't Malik's, why did you take it with you when you ran out? I want to see it."

"Um...no. I lost it in the woods. I grabbed it from the trash because I didn't want anyone to find it. It was too personal." My voice wavers, and I stop talking before I crumble from the pressure building up. The walls are closing in, and I'm trapped.

Olive speaks up. "Ms. Simmons, I'm wondering if you would allow me and Rocky some time to find out the truth about what really happened to the missing papers? We have some experience as master sleuths."

I might not go that far to describe us, but last year we did crack a major secret about how my dad died. There's no better problem-solver than Olive.

I say, "Maybe you could give us a couple of hours? We'll find out who the real culprit is. Please. It's my life on the line here."

Every organ in me halts its functioning, waiting for her decision. Even if we get the time, there's no guarantee we'll be successful, but I have to try.

"Okay, I'll give you two hours," Ms. Simmons says, "but I will not accept any explanation you can't prove."

I do a quick fist pump. "Yes! I understand. Thank you, Ms. Simmons. Let's go, Olive."

I grab her hand and pull her out the door.

CHAPTER 28

Once we're outside, Olive doesn't waste a second. "Rocky, spill now—do not omit a single detail about that day, no matter how insignificant it seems."

"I'm so glad you're here," I start, "I was afraid you might ditch me when you discovered what they're saying I did." I think it is too weird to share the hologram story with her. Best to keep that to myself.

"Oh, Rocket Man, you can be as dense as the forest. Why would you think that? Talk already and talk fast. There must be some clue you missed."

"My backpack was on the floor between Ted and me at the reading, and he had plenty of time to steal Malik's papers when I was at the podium."

"Why would he do that unless you gave him the impression you would agree to anything so you could win, and he took it literally? Maybe he even thought you were asking him to sort of sucker punch the kid for you."

"I mentioned that one kid would be tough competition, and if he wasn't at Lakeside, I'd have a better chance at the top prize, but I never asked Ted to do anything. Here's the play-by-play. That afterno—"

Ted jogs over to us and interrupts. "I want to help you two

prove Rocky's innocence, and whatever you do, Rocky, do not give a false confession."

Is this just Ted's way of showing off for Mom so he can act like my savior?

"Ted, it's not a good idea for you to come with us. And you know why," I answer.

"No, I don't know why."

This is the perfect opening for me to tell him my suspicion. "Because you have been—"

Olive cuts me off and says, "Gosh, Ted, you've been so nice, but Rocky's mother needs you now. You should be with her. Let Rocky and me work on this, and we'll keep you in the loop."

Olive gives me a weird grin, which I think translates into "shut up, Rocky." After the horror of her hologram getting so angry with me, I'm not doing anything to upset her.

"Yes, that makes sense. If you're sure you're okay, Rocky?" Ted asks.

I glance at Olive and know what I have to say. "I'm sure."

Ted goes back to the office, and Olive says, "Rocky, he's really trying."

"Maybe." I remember thinking his oddball expressions were kinda humorous before the word *marriage* was spoken. After that nothing he did seemed funny or harmless anymore.

"Start from the very beginning," she orders.

I begin with the afternoon of the reading, when Malik and I were revising our stories, and finish with his injury in the woods. Throughout my recitation, Olive remains silent.

"That's it," I say. "There's nothing more. It's hopeless." I kick the dirt under my feet into a small dust cloud that floats a few inches off the ground.

"Enough with the depressing talk. You give up too easily. Let's check out the log cabin. Maybe the kid lost his papers on his way up to read."

"Okay." Olive dispenses hope like a soap dispenser dispenses soap. Ha. Ha. Soap is a good metaphor because she's always cleaning up my messes. I give myself applause that through all this I haven't lost my awesome sense of humor.

Inside the log cabin, Olive walks down the middle of the room and says, "This is our dividing line. You search that half, and I'll do this side. Check the shelves along the wall and the wastebaskets. The missing pages could be anywhere."

Olive and I slow-walk the space. My eyes scan every angle of the room from floor to ceiling. For the first time, I touch the filling between the logs that seems mushy enough to hide some stolen papers. It is hard. *Duh, Rocky, if that stuff was soft the whole building would collapse.* I should ask Ted how they build log cabins. A construction guy like him would know.

I check the area around the podium while Olive opens cabinets filled with the dishes and other dining hall stuff. All the wastebaskets are empty.

"I'm sinking fast," I say.

"Buck up, Rocky. We've just started. Where's your backpack, anyway?"

"I ran out and left it. It's not here now. Althea might've have taken it with her."

"Okay, let's go find this Althea, and you can fill me in along the way about who she is."

"She's at the grove. Morning workshops are in session."

"To the grove," Olive says with the sureness of a commander-in-chief directing the troops.

As we walk, I describe Althea in all her gloriousness.

"You're in love with her," Olive teases.

I must come off like a crazy fan-boy. My face heats up.

"Uh...no," I say, but who am I fooling? She's right. Olive smirks, but when she lays eyes on Althea, she'll understand.

"Describe the kid who lost his papers."

"Why?" I ask, not sure where she's going with this.

"Maybe he's the type to pull a stunt like this and throw you under the bus so you would get booted out and he'd win by default, or else he might be covering up for the fact he never finished writing his story."

Wow. Malik might be a bragger and sometimes obnoxious, but I doubt he'd do that, even though winning the national prize for him would be like scoring a Super Bowl ring. I can picture Malik riding on a float above the crowds on the streets of Manhattan as everyone, including his dad, cheers his victory.

"This guy is intent on winning, and he's a great writer, but he doesn't need any tricks to have a chance at the top prize. I don't think he'd do anything that despicable," I say, defending Malik. Things are different between us after our tough night in the woods together. Why is that I could reconsider my initial impression about Malik, but I'm not willing to do the same for Ted? Double standard, I guess.

Olive continues, "Sometimes things get mixed up, and the people you don't suspect of an evil deed might be capable of something awful; and those you're sure do bad stuff, haven't done anything wrong. I bet this kid is no saint. No one is, but I'll reserve judgment on him until I can eyeball him directly."

"He's sort of arrogant and a bit full of himself. His mother treats him like a god because he's such a genius."

"So, do we like him or not, Rocket Man?"

"TBD," I reply.

CHAPTER 23

On any other day, I'd be excited to show off the grove to Olive so she could bask in the peacefulness of this place, but today peace and I are complete strangers.

"Olive, we can't stay here long or we'll run out of time."

"Uh-huh," she says, not paying attention because she's too busy staring at Althea. Not surprised. And today, Althea's outfit doesn't disappoint. Her green pants sway as she strolls back and forth, and she wears a multicolored turban like a crown. As always, she's amazing.

"She's your teacher?" Olive asks as soon as her brain kicks back into gear.

"She's a famous author and more like a mentor."

"She's gorgeous. Do you see how the sun makes the gold threads in her outfit sparkly?"

That's too much fashion detail for me.

Althea spots us and says, "Rocky, I wasn't sure you would be in the workshop today."

"Er ... I can't stay," I mumble.

"Good, because we don't want you here, story-thief," Chloe says, with a hint of spit in each corner of her mouth.

"I'm not a thief. I mean, I didn't do it," I say.

Isabelle joins Chloe in scolding me, saying, "You lucked out that Malik will be okay."

JJ, as usual, comes to my rescue and stands up to fist bump me. "Hey, dude, don't listen to them. The dust in their eyes clouds their minds when precious Maliky, the boy who can do no wrong, is involved."

Problem is, I do understand their anger.

Olive is in a trance, and if she doesn't shake it Althea might have her arrested as a stalker-type.

"Who are you?" Chloe asks, turning her attention to Olive with a scowl, as if Olive has no right to be here.

"She's my girlfriend," I explain, which I think describes what we are. I hope Olive doesn't object to me calling her that in front of everyone.

"Well, la-di-da. Good for you. You have a girlfriend." Chloe speaks with thick sarcasm. Then, to make sure I get her message she fish claps at me. Rude. But she's so in love with Malik, I guess I can't expect her to be rational. She would never be willing to consider my side of this.

Althea says, "Listen, Malik wouldn't be the first writer to lose his work. Years ago, before I published my first novel, I wrote a short story for a contest. I was sure a win would help put me on the map with agents before I queried them.

Isabelle asks, "What happened to your story?"

"My computer crashed. In those days, I didn't use an external hard drive backup. There was no Dropbox or Cloud, so I lost everything."

Chloe asks, "Couldn't you rewrite it?"

"I tried, but the new version was inferior."

"But you're a best-selling author," Isabelle says, stating the obvious.

"I queried my novel anyway, hoping I could succeed without the contest, and I lucked out. Three agents gave me offers, but I still remember how gut wrenching it was when my story disappeared. It taught me a lesson. There's nothing worse for a writer."

Does she think I don't know how awful it must be to lose your work? Is she trying to make me feel even lower than a worm? I want to cover my ears so I can't hear my deafening heartbeats. Wish there was a magic way for me to disappear right now.

Finally, Olive snaps out of her Althea reverie and says, "We're looking for Rocky's backpack. Did any of you take it from the log cabin last night?"

"No," Isabelle says.

"Are you sure? This is a matter of life and death," I say.

"Save your exaggerations for your fiction. You aren't going to death row," Isabelle snarks.

Chloe high-fives her, and JJ freezes his eyes mid-roll. Those girls are too much for him. I feel him.

"I recall Ted saying he was going to bring it to your cabin when the program was over," Althea says. "Did you ask him? Rocky, I'm sure there is a simple explanation for what happened. I, for one, do not believe you would do something like that."

Nice to hear a vote of confidence from Althea. That means a lot. I hope she stuck up for me with Ms. Simmons, too.

"Because of what happened, Malik should get the top prize," Chloe proposes.

"That's not how this works, Chloe," Althea explains. "We have to consider all your work this summer and not just one presentation."

Olive clutches my hand and drags me off, saying, "We should check your room now."

We walk away as Isabelle's annoying voice booms out, "You're just jealous of Malik."

Does everybody see that in me? Jealousy isn't a good look. But even so, that doesn't mean I'd deliberately hurt his chances at the prize. I'm tired of defending myself and say, "Let's forget this, Olive. I'll throw myself on Ms. Simmons's mercy, if she has any, and this nightmare will be over. Mom will stand behind me."

"Ted will, too," Olive adds.

"Still don't trust him."

"Ted is convinced you're innocent. Didn't you listen when he offered to help? Rocky, you're caught up in developing your case against him, and it's making you dense to see what's real. I like Ted."

Anger roils inside my core. I say, "How can you like Ted? You can't like both of us. That's being a traitor. You have to choose. You know, when I searched Ted's room I found something very suspicious. He has a T-shirt with the same college logo where my dad went to school. Why would Ted have that? Unless he's planning to pretend he's my father."

"Listen to yourself," Olive says. "Your mom wouldn't fall for someone so devious. I admit it's odd he has that same shirt, but your mom didn't have to choose between the two of you, or I guess she chose both of you."

Olive is making my head hurt. I just keep getting buried in a fresh load of crap. It's odd how when one thing goes wrong, another follows it like life is a long domino train collapsing in a continuous sequence.

I walk absorbed in my own sorry little world and don't notice for a while that Olive isn't beside me. When I do, I turn and see her standing a few yards back with arms folded across her chest and a gaze that punctures me harsher than her hologram did when it dumped me.

"And do not call me a traitor," she says. "That girl in your workshop might be on to something. You might be suffering from a serious case of jealousy-disease when it comes to Malik and Ted. Instead of writing, you should consider going to medical school to develop a vaccine for that. You need to get your head straight. I'm outta here."

She pivots to head back and leaves me standing there. It's as if the sun stopped shining, and the temperature plummeted to one hundred degrees below zero. I wish I had time to run after her, but I have to finish my search. There's so much at stake. I keep going to the cabin to find my backpack.

My hand trembles as I turn the handle on the door and say under my breath, "This is my last chance."

Yosh and Luke are perched on their beds sketching like always, and from their shocked faces I doubt they expected to see me again.

Yosh says, "I'm surprised you have the guts to return after what you did."

"I didn't do anything," I say, exhausted from repeating that phrase. What's the point? No one believes me. I'm not even sure I believe me anymore. I could confess and end this, even though I'll be marked for life.

"So you claim you're innocent?" Yosh says,

"I'm claiming it because it's true, and I will prove it." That last bit is way over confident, and I strongly doubt my chances for success.

"When is Malik coming back?" Luke pipes up.

"Soon. Ms. Simmons says he'll be fine. Is my backpack here?"

Yosh says, "We brought it back and threw it under the bed so it could live with the dust bunnies."

I get down on all fours, pull out the backpack and brush it off.

Yosh flings his arm around Luke and says, "Lukey, let's go."

Halfway out the door, Luke steps back in and says, "Good luck, Rocky."

Luke's gesture surprises me. Maybe he has reevaluated his initial assumption about my guilt, and his comment seems to give Yosh permission to ease up on me too. Luke gives me a tiny hug. Some guys are queasy about hugging another guy, but I have no problem with it. I guess I'm forgiven, or almost forgiven.

"Thanks, I needed that," I say.

"I draw faces all day long, and your eyes don't look guilty," Luke announces. "It's difficult to hide a guilty look."

Yosh interrupts, "If this artist thing doesn't work out for you, bro, you could be a judge and inspect the suspect's eyes to decide guilt or innocence. We could get rid of the lawyers and juries."

I agree and say, "Yup, Luke's the boy with the magic eyes. Sees all. Knows all."

They leave, and I open the backpack and dump the contents on the floor. The only papers in there are mine. I don't bother putting anything back. I check the cubbies in case someone stuffed the papers in there. As I get to the last shelf, the door squeaks open, and I assume Yosh and Luke are returning.

"I'm almost done," I say, without looking up.

"Done with what?" Malik asks.

CHAPTER 30

Malik hobbles in on crutches, and Ted trails behind him. The bandage on Malik's leg is thick and the wrong color for his skin. Heck, what's the matter with those medical people? Can't they just make green bandages to match the color of outer-space aliens for everyone.

Despite what the guy's been through, Malik is still studly with glowing eyes and gleaming teeth which are offset by his deep reddish lips.

"Hi, Rocky," Ted says.

I wave to him.

"I walked Malik back to make sure he could navigate with the crutches."

"Hey, Malik, how are you feeling?" I ask.

"Much better. I'm full of antibiotics and other medicine."

"It must've been brutal when they removed the stick."

"They shot me with numbing stuff. I could still feel a ton of pressure on my leg as if they all sat on it."

"Did it gush again?"

"I was too afraid to look," he says and adds, "and thank you, by the way."

Ted gives Malik a pat on the back.

I'm confused. "Why are you thanking me," I ask, "I'm the guy responsible for all your problems?"

"Not all of them. The branch-in-the-leg thing is on me, and you risked a lot to make sure I got to a doctor. My injury impressed the people at the hospital. They took lots of photos before and after they removed the branch and said I was lucky it didn't go clear through. They marveled at my amazing ability to fall at the precise angle so I would land on a broken branch that was positioned on the ground also at the perfect angle to stab me. A doctor told me this accident was one in a million, and it might be in the medical books someday. I'll be famous for my injury. My writing will have to play catchup to equal that achievement."

Malik, who once seemed allergic to cracking a joke, has developed a sense of humor or it's the meds talking.

"I'm glad you'll be okay."

"What are you doing here?" he asks.

"Looking for your papers."

"They couldn't be here. I put them in your backpack, remember?"

"But what if you didn't?"

"Impossible."

Ted interrupts and says he has to get back to Mom because she's suffering from a severe case of mom-jitters. For the first time, I'm kinda glad he'll be with her so she won't be alone.

"Thanks for walking with me to the cabin, Ted."

When it's just the two of us, Malik says, "I love that dude's beard. I'm growing a soul patch as soon as I can." Malik pats the place under his lower lip where he hopes some hair will grow.

If Malik thinks that beard is fashionable, then it must be cool. Perhaps I might've been too judgmenty about Ted's looks, but I still have plenty of other issues to take up with that guy.

Malik says, "Wait until my mother sees my leg. She'll throw

a fit if I'm left with a whopping scar. How will she cope with a son with a defect?"

"Hilarious," I say. "You're still the best-looking guy ever."

In a high-pitched shriek he imitates his mom: "Oh, my beautiful boy, my gorgeous Malik."

"Ha. Ha."

"Rocky, will you put the crutches away and help me get into bed? I'm exhausted."

I prop his crutches in the corner of the room, plump his pillow and pull down the blankets so he can slide underneath. There, under the sheet, wedged between the bed frame and the wall, are two pieces of paper. *Two pieces of paper!* I stare, afraid that if I touch them, they might crumble or turn out to be some trick my mind is playing on me. My tongue sticks to the roof of my mouth, and I can't speak.

"What's the holdup?" Malik asks and limps up beside me. If this isn't my imagination, he'll see the papers too. I watch as his eyes track mine and settle on the papers. Unlike me, he isn't scared to grab them.

"It's my story. The missing pages. In my own bed. How could that happen?"

"Dunno" is my feeble response, but there must be an explanation. The papers didn't get there by themselves.

"I've got to sit down," Malik says and parks his butt on the bed. "Rocky, you know as well as I do we were writing on our beds all afternoon.

"Who else was in the room?" I ask.

"Yosh and Luke. Then Ted came in to replace some burnt-out bulbs."

Ted! I knew it! Ted's behind everything that goes wrong in my life.

"Ted was gone by the time we got back from the bathroom, but someone had fixed my bed so it wasn't such a jumble of sheets and blankets. Then we changed clothes. I picked up my papers, and we left."

So, while we were showering, Ted must've made Malik's bed and hid a couple of pages of his story. So bold. So bad.

"I guess when I gave you my story to put inside your backpack for protection, I must not have had all of it with me."

I can't take my eyes off the papers he's holding as if there are taser wires emitting a strong current connecting me to them. I ask, "Did you check you had all the pages when we left?"

"No, I just assumed they were all there. Rocky, I'm so sorry. My bad."

"Just wow," I say. Yosh and Luke might have the answers if they noticed anything suspicious when Ted was straightening out Malik's bed. But first we have to tell Ms. Simmons so I can clear my name.

Malik cannot stop apologizing. "I accused you with no proof. I'm such an idiot. Can you forgive me?"

"I would've come to the same conclusion if it was the other way around. Are you able to walk with me to the office? You should be the one to tell Ms. Simmons what happened."

"Yes, but I'm slow on the crutches," Malik says.

"Who cares about slow? I'm about to get my life back."

CHAPTER 31

O ur turtle's pace to the office seems endless, but I squash all temptation to run ahead.

"Malik, did you know the national soccer team trains in L.A.?"

"And why would I care about that?"

"When you get there, it might be interesting to check out where they practice. It could be an inspiration for a new story about soccer players who are really gladiators. Could be funny to have them ride into the stadium on horses."

Malik pauses to rest, which makes me antsy, but I'm relieved to see the wayward papers poking out of his pocket. He brought the proof.

"I do love horses, but I don't love sports," Malik says.

"Here's my idea. When you win the trip, you can ask your dad to go with you to Los Angeles. There are lots of cool things to do there."

"Not sure he'd want to go with me, and I may not win," Malik says. In a strange way having a branch in his leg has corked some of his over-the-top bragging.

I continue describing my terrific plan for him. "And if you two are away, your mom will have to give special attention to your brothers. This would be a win-win for everyone."

Of course, if he gets the prize that means I won't, and my chance to make Dad's and my dream to see the training center come true ends. But without Dad, it probably would be way too depressing anyway. I know soccer fields won't mean much to Malik, but they might interest his sports-loving father. Plus, a trip like that is good quality time with his dad. I'd love to be able to have that. I'm proud of my excellent advice. If I don't become a lawyer or a detective, I might have a future as a life coach.

We start walking again, and I wonder if they moved the office a mile away while we were in the cabin. We finally get there, and Olive, Mom, and Ted are sitting on a bench at a picnic table.

Mom says, "I was worried when Olive returned without you, but Ted said you were okay."

Olive's eyes twinkle, and her smile puffs out across her face, which must mean I'm no longer in her dungeon. But on closer examination, her glorious gaze is for Malik and not me. She has the same dumb expression Isabelle and Chloe get whenever that boy is nearby.

I'm tempted to shake her and say, "Look at me. I'm here too."

Mom introduces herself to Malik, and I hold the office door open. We crowd into the tiny space, and this time, Malik and I are the ones who sit. Ted stows the crutches.

"Ms. Simmons," Malik says, "What happened wasn't Rocky's fault. It's mine. He never had all the pages of my story in his backpack. Some of my papers got tucked under the blankets on my bed. I'm truly sorry." Malik reaches into the big pocket of his cargo shorts and hands the wayward papers to Ms. Simmons.

She studies them and then eyeballs each of us for a moment. A loud hiss fills the quiet space. I look around and realize that noise is coming from my own lungs. I'm squeezing out a long exhale that will require a big swig of oxygen to refill my empty reservoir.

Malik can't stop talking. "I never brought them to the reading and never put them in his backpack. I panicked when they were missing. I couldn't see any other possibility except that Rocky took them so I'd bomb. I let a misguided suspicion cloud my thinking."

Boy, that's what I do when I'm on the alert about Ted's suspicious behavior. Malik's eyes fill up, and I don't want him to lose it in front of everyone, so I jump in and say, "I would've done the same thing in his shoes. Case closed. I'm not angry, not in the slightest."

Many hands come from behind my chair and clap me on the back in approval.

Ms. Simmons returns Malik's pages to him, picks up the letters she wrote to my school, and rips them into pieces before tossing them in the wastebasket. She says, "Marybeth, you and Rocky's friend are welcome to stay for the final readings and the awards ceremony tomorrow."

"Thank you," Mom replies and stretches out her hand to Ms. Simmons. "I would love to. I'll call Olive's parents to get their okay."

When we exit the office, Ted sneaks up beside me. "I reassured your mother this would have a happy conclusion. I had a hunch you would find the papers."

"How could you know that? Unless—" Can this guy be so dumb he would admit knowing how this episode would end? I've caught him now.

"Unless what?" he asks.

"The two of us need to talk. Alone. And do not tell Mom."

"Okay," Ted agrees. I doubt he's aware what I've got in store for him.

"Wait here until I talk to Olive."

"Okay," he says again. I sense my power over him growing.

Olive is still yakking it up with Malik. I come up beside her and give her a gentle shove so she'll look at me.

It works. "What is it?" she asks, a bit annoyed that I interrupted whatever was going on.

"I need help," I say.

"What else is new? Okay. Got to go, Malik. See you later," she says.

She and I move away from the others. I ask her, "Are you still mad at me? I'm sorry I called you a traitor. You have to help me figure out how to get Ted alone to grill him without alerting my mom. This has to go under her radar."

Olive tilts her head from one side to the other, as if that movement helps stir up her brain matter so she can think. I don't interrupt her process.

"Got it," she says, all glowy with her customary confidence.

"Ask Ted to help you do something in your room. Your mom will offer to come too, so you need to tell her no females allowed in a boys' room. Make sense?"

Does she even have to ask that? The thing about Olive's schemes is that once she gives you the deets, you're mad at yourself for not coming up with it yourself. She makes it seem so amazingly simple. We walk back to where Mom and Ted are in deep convo.

I start by saying, "Ted, when I was searching for the papers in my room, I made a giant mess. It'll take me forever to clean up by myself. Can you help?"

"Why don't I do that, sweetheart? You've had a tough day," Mom says, right on cue, as if Olive had programmed her. "Olive and I would love to help, wouldn't we?"

Boy, is my mom predictable.

"Sure," Olive says and kind of scrunches her nose up and down in a signal as if she's giving me silent stage directions.

"No females in the room now, Mom. The guys wouldn't like it. Just Ted."

"Oh, I should've realized that," she says, backing off.

Ted says, "Sure, bud—, guy—, dud—. Er...Rocky." Poor Ted. He's so befuddled. I've got him off balance just where I want him.

Zero hour has arrived, and the inquisition will begin.

CHAPTER 32

"We're going to your room to talk," I tell him when we're away from the others. For once my vocal cords cooperate, and I don't sound like a little kid. He has to know who's in charge here.

We hike up the hill to the staff area, and Ted chatters nervously. "I'm sure the end of the program will be terrific. Everything happens as it should." His predictions about the future, my future, are eerie. What kind of power allows this guy to think he knows everything?

Once we're inside his room, Ted clams up, and his eyebrows move into full rollercoaster mode like he has no control over them. He seems nervous, probably senses his back is against the wall as if he's facing a firing squad. And I'm the one who will give the order to shoot.

"Before you start, Rocky, I have something to say. I won't marry your mom if you're not okay with it."

Holy Moley! I was not expecting that. His promise is like money in the bank. I may yet need it. It could be a game changer.

"Here's the deal," I say, "I'm not convinced I can trust you, but I owe it to my mom to give you a shot."

"I will prove you can trust me." Ted plunks down on his bed

as if his legs are too weak to hold up his weight. Suddenly, he looks tired, and I haven't even started in on him yet. I'm wearing him down like a boxer who has his opponent hanging on the ropes and then unleashes the final right hook.

Ted motions for me to sit on the lone chair in the corner, but I don't. Everyone knows that standing is the command position.

I begin. "You came to my soccer game, which you claimed was your first, but you were arrogant enough to tell me how to play from the bleachers. What you said about the direction of the ball was in direct contradiction to what I saw in front of me, and yet you turned out to be right. I made the opposite move, and it cost my team the game. How did you make that kick go to the left?"

"Are you asking if I waved a magic wand over the ball? You can't be serious."

I don't reply because I'm using a technique that I learned from police shows when the cop keeps quiet after asking a question, tricking the suspect into filling the silence by spilling his guts.

It works. Ted keeps talking. "I didn't make that player do anything. The kid stopped the ball and switched feet right before he kicked. I guess he's ambidextrous with his feet. He tried to fake you out, so I wanted to give you a heads-up."

I replay the scene, visualizing the kid dribbling down the field toward me and setting the ball for his shot. If he shifted his feet at the last second, it would explain the change in direction, but by then I was already in motion flinging my body to the other side. Only a few players have that skill to change their kicking foot. It's like putting down a perfect and unexpected bunt in baseball. The element of surprise is dynamite in any game.

"That might be possible," I admit. "Though it's extremely unusual. Okay, let's say I accept your explanation. What about your hunch that I'd go to Lakeside instead of soccer camp? The very next day I broke my foot as if you arranged the whole thing so you could make your hunch come true. How did you manage that?"

"Do you think I made you break your foot? That's preposterous! I spoke to Coach Taylor a few days after it happened to thank him for taking great care of you. He told me the maintenance crew at the field had called to apologize because they had re-sodded the area near the goal a short time before the game. The dirt was still damp and not firmly packed. As soon as your cleat caught a chunk, down you went. And the reason I talked up your scholarship to Lakeside was because it was a major achievement and that was my way of saying I was proud of you."

This isn't going as planned. I start to pace but soon feel dizzy having to make continuous about-face turns in this cramped space and plop on the chair. But I'm not finished with him. My grilling continues. "Why did you mess with my roommates' clothes and not mine, leaving me to take the blame for that?"

"You can't believe I would do that." He is wide-eyed, fixated on me as if I'm an alien creature who emerged from some mysterious slime pool and is both scary and curious.

"Well, maybe I *can* believe it," I say.

"Just last night Jono was bragging about all the pranks he pulled this summer, including the one in your room. He said that before he could finish his dumb deed, you guys came back, and he had to make a quick exit, leaving his dirty work incomplete. Personally, I find him to be a donkey's rear end. He's so smug. If I'd known he did it sooner, I would've told you."

Jono? Could be. I wouldn't put it past a guy like that who's wavering between full-scale delinquent or perfecting his amateur status as a troublemaker. But I never suspected him, because I was sure it had to be Ted.

Ted has plausible answers for everything, which either means he's telling the truth, or he's a well-rehearsed professional liar who can make up stuff on the spot.

Time to fire the big guns. "Why did you hide Malik's papers?"

"I didn't do that." His butt rises a few inches off the bed as if my question lifts his whole body, but he settles back down. "I would never do anything like that. I can't believe you would think I did."

"While Malik and I were showering, you were changing the bulb. Remember?"

"So?"

"So, Malik left his papers, and when you straightened his bed, you hid two pages under the sheet."

Ted laughs. "Oh, no. Really? That's where they were? That's a strange occurrence. But it wasn't me. While I was in the room, Yosh told Luke he was going to make Malik's bed so Malik wouldn't have to come back to such a mess after the reading. I'm sure Yosh didn't hide the papers on purpose. Most likely, he didn't pay any attention to them." Ted smiles. "It's kind of random that they could get caught up in the sheets."

Whatever negative opinion I had about Ted, he isn't the type to throw Yoshiki under the bus. And Yosh would be bummed to learn he's responsible for this whole fiasco. I'm sure he didn't mean for any of this to happen.

This isn't going as expected, but I have one last pitch to hurl at Ted. "Okay, let's forget about that. Why did you give me a suitcase and say I would take a trip? Right after that I slipped on the auditorium steps, and Max said, 'Nice trip, Rocky.' You wanted me to fall, didn't you?"

"Of course not. The trip I was referring to had nothing to do with you taking a tumble in school. I was hinting at something else."

"But I'm not going anywhere."

Ted stammers a lot of hmmms, ohs, and ers. Clearly, he's searching for a way to cover his you-know-what. This time he has no quick explanation. I may have finally trapped him. I'm gonna make him sweat this.

A moment passes before he decides he can speak. "I'll tell you what I meant, but you have to promise not to breathe a word to your mom. I mean it. If she finds out I told you, I'm dead. Can I trust you not to snitch?"

Boom! Gotcha! I shout in my head. Now I've caught him, and he's squirming like the lizard he is. His hands run back and forth through his hair in a sort of nervous tic kind of way. In other circumstances, I'd take pity on him, but not when I'm about to squeeze the truth out of him.

"The new suitcase is for a trip for the three of us. Your mom is planning to tell you after the ceremony. Now I've spoiled it."

This could be his version of fake news. People don't take their kids on their honeymoon, so I say, "Don't believe you. You're kidding."

"I'm not. We're going to Universal Orlando: Harry Potter World and maybe we'll hit up the ESPN World of Sports at Disney."

My lower lip drops as if anchors are attached at each end. Boy, have I been a nitwit about a lot of things! Ted was evil in my mind, so I fit all the bad stuff that happened to me into a plot against him. I misinterpreted everything just like Malik did about me when he couldn't find the rest of his story.

"You're kidding," I repeat.

"Please don't tell. It will upset your mom I told you without her."

Still unsure if I should accept his explanation as

percent true, I ask, "And you didn't want to go on your honeymoon just with Mom?"

"No way. We want you to be with us. It's a familymoon. Funny, huh?"

"I'm embarrassed that I imagined you could cast spells on me, but I never figured out the 'why' part of that theory which now seems so ridiculous." I continue to unload all the stupid stuff I have built up in my mind. "I even suspected you used some black magic to control that bird so it would poop only on me." I smile, aware of how outrageous that sounds.

But instead of returning my smile, Ted crosses his legs, and his foot twitches wildly. Looks like some major anxiety. Now what have I done?

He says, "I must have seemed like a typical comic book villain who descended on you to wreak havoc. So distressing for you."

"I wasn't willing to give you the benefit of the doubt," I say. "I judged you, but it was a wrongful conviction. There's nothing worse than sending someone to prison for a crime they didn't commit, or for breaking up you and Mom for no decent reason."

His foot doesn't stop moving, and there's no sign from him we're in an okay place. His expression freezes as if his face was dipped in ice and even his crazy eyebrows have stopped their perpetual motion.

"It's not as simple as that," he replies.

CHAPTER 33

W hat isn't simple? I suck back my last exhale in case I need that air for extra lung capacity so I can make a quick getaway.

Ted lowers his head, and I'm left staring at a hunk of black hair. I almost miss those thick, wayward eyebrows of his. Something is wrong, and I'm scared to find out what.

Courage, Rocky. "Is it about me?" I ask.

"Yes."

Not the answer I wanted. If he ends the relationship with Mom on account of me, I'll never be able to make that up to her. No doubt she's way happier when he's around. I stare at him but still have no visual on his face. It's amazing how much we rely on facial expressions to understand where we stand with people.

"What did I do?" I ask.

"You didn't do anything."

"But you just said it's about me."

As if someone yanked on his puppet strings, he raises his head, and his eyes dart from side to side to avoid landing them directly on me.

"It's about what you might do. If you tell your mom not to marry me, she won't. So, there's a lot riding on this."

"I'm past that. You aren't the wicked wizard or the evil Darth Vader." I laugh.

In a feeble voice, as if he's drawing his last breath on his deathbed, Ted says, "You were correct to have suspicions about me because I'm keeping a secret from you. I wanted to tell you the truth so many times, but things kept happening that were tough for you, and I didn't want to pile on."

A month ago, heck, even an hour ago, this would be an aha moment. Now it's like he's struggling to climb out of an oily well and keeps falling back in. I throw him a lifeline with a lie. "Your secret is safe with me," I say, but the truth is if I have to protect Mom, I'll give him up in a heartbeat.

He lifts his head and says, "Here it is: your dad was a friend of mine in college." Then the puppeteer loses his grip and his head slides back down. I sense my eyes growing like rolling snowballs with a spot of blue ice in the center. I'm dumbfounded, mind-muddled, stunned, confused. The hunt for synonyms drains me, so I quit doing that.

"My dad!" At last, I cough up two words before my mouth goes desert-dry.

He continues, "I didn't make the connection at first. It had been so many years since I had any contact with Ron. I didn't know he had died. It wasn't until I went to your house and came across the photos of your dad and then your mom shared some details about him, and it added up. I realized your dad had been my old college friend. At first, I was afraid your mom might think I was some kind of a creepy stalker who dated her only because she was Ron's widow."

I swish my tongue around to unleash some saliva so I can speak. "What did my mom say when you told her?"

He glances up with the barest glimmer of a smile. "She was surprised but decided it was a positive sign because your dad had liked me. Do you think that's strange?"

"Why didn't she tell me about this?"

"I asked her if I could do it so the two of us could begin our relationship with honesty. She agreed. Then, my nervousness took over and prevented me from finding the exact right moment. I became an expert procrastinator."

Secrets and I have a troubled past. They can leave scars and bring unintended consequences. They must be opened before they become poisonous.

"When was the last time you saw my dad?"

"We lost touch while I was on a semester abroad in England. When I returned, he had eloped. Remember when I said your mom and I didn't want to elope, and I tried to backpedal that remark in case you took it as a criticism about how your parents got married?"

I never put that together.

As Ted continues to talk, his facial muscles begin to relax, and he appears more normal. Normal for him, that is. "Also, I let it slip how one of your expressions was like Ron's. I covered my mistake by blaming it on the photo in your room, which had nothing to do with my memory. But sometimes you make a face that reminds me of your dad."

That had also flown right over my head.

"And your dad once told me he wanted to be a professional soccer player, but that was before he met Marybeth."

It must've been strange for Ted to have Dad lurking in his mind while he's dating Mom. I feel some compassion for him and move to sit next to him on the bed. I even place my arm lightly around his shoulder. It's weird to touch him and strange that he doesn't even respond. Mom might have been right; he's scared of me.

"Should we go find your mom?" He asks and gets up, but I stay put.

"I also have not been totally truthful. It's my turn for a full confession."

"Huh?"

"I was the one who broke into your room to snoop. Sorry."

"Oh, wow. I never suspected it was you."

"I was nosing around for evidence so I could convince Mom to call off the wedding. What are you doing with a soccer book under your bed?"

"Oh, that. I'm studying the rules so I won't be the dummy in the stands at your varsity games, if I'm allowed to come."

"And I once peeked in your wallet because I wanted to google you and didn't know your last name. Sorry, again. I found a photo of you and another woman, who isn't my mother, with two kids."

His dark eyes gleam, but there's nothing sinister in them. "I can understand how that might've looked suspicious. She's my sister, Jeanie, and those are her kids. I hope she'll come to the wedding, if there still is one."

I swallow a mouthful of stupidity, which tastes worse than anything Professor Snape might brew. I did to Ted what Malik did to me, only believing the worst things about him. That kind of stinks.

"I'm ready now. Let's go," I say.

Together, we step into the sun. I look up and close my eyes for a sec letting the warmth soothe me. In the last half hour, life has changed. It is so much better. Ted puts one foot in front of the other gingerly as if he only recently learned how to walk, but soon enough he regains his confidence, and we pick up the pace.

Now I must find Olive to get me out of my newest predicament. I can't read my final story at the award presentation tomorrow.

CHAPTER 34

I wish my life was as smooth as Mr. Maxwell's rowing on the lake, but unfortunately, you have to constantly make adjustments and adapt. That's my new theory. It's a challenge for sure.

Ted must sense I'm on edge, and he asks, "Are you okay? You seem upset. I thought things were better." He has picked up on my worry vibe.

"They are better." I don't want him to pepper me with more questions so I change the subject. "Were you in my dad's fraternity, too?"

"Yes. How did you know that?"

"I found your college shirt with the Greek letters. My dad had the same one. I suspected that you bought it to pretend you're my father. Seeing that T-shirt in your drawer set my eyeballs on fire."

"You were thorough in your investigation, but I promise I never think I'm your dad. I want to be your good friend, and I want you to trust me."

"That wasn't my first time snooping. I'm ashamed to admit I once scoured my mom's room for clues about how my dad died. But I swear, on my word of honor, when you two get married,

I'll retire permanently from all amateur detective work, including eavesdropping and spying."

As we walk, I realize that not once has Ted unleashed a bunch of silly sayings about Dad like others have. Some people thought they had to tell me what a great guy my dad was as if I was too dumb to know that. Ted has screwy expressions, but he never said anything hurtful.

Mom might be right that if Dad and Ted were friends, Dad must've liked him. It's almost like Dad has given his blessing to this marriage, assuming a first husband is allowed to do that for the second one.

Ted and I find Olive and Mom near the parking lot. Ted's eyebrows signal his delight when he spots Mom, who responds with a mile-long smile. I'll have to get used to the way they have their own language, but I might need a little more time to tamp down some lingering embers of jealousy. I know I'm not always going to be at the center of her life.

Mom slips her arm through mine. "I made arrangements for a motel room for Olive and me for tonight. Isn't that great? We'll be at the reading and awards ceremony tomorrow."

That is not great! I was gonna try to figure out a way to leave today by pretending I had to start training for soccer. Now I have to stay even though I have nothing to read at the presentation.

Olive takes a swig of cola, and I reach into the cooler for a water. Coach Taylor is strict about sugary drinks, and I'm already preparing for the season. I'm tempted to empty the bottle over my head to cool off, but instead I rub the damp plastic across my forehead.

Also, if I leave here early, everyone at Lakeside might think I'm running away again. This problem requires solving by the brilliant queen of schemes, aka Olive.

"The guys said it was okay for me to bring Olive to our cabin. They want to meet her."

"That's nice," Mom responds.

Olive's eyes narrow into questioning slivers because she suspects I am faking about the guys wanting to meet her. She knows me well.

"You two go ahead. We'll catch you later," Mom says.

As soon as we're on the path, Olive asks, "Wassup?"

"I can't read my story tomorrow."

"Why not?"

"It's not my best work." But it really is. Althea loves my story and said it was full of suspense with dark themes. She told me I have a genuine talent for sci-fi. Her praise is like winning a gold medal.

"Ah, no. My you-know-what meter is registering that statement false," Olive says as she moves her index finger in a semicircle from left to right like it's a pointer on a meter and adds a buzzing noise indicating wrong answer.

"So mysterious, you are. A regular Yoda, you seem," she says, which makes me chuckle-groan.

"Everything has changed. Ted is an okay dude, and all my accusations had logical explanations. You tried to tell me it was all in my head, but I wouldn't listen because I was intent on breaking them up. And there's other news: Ted and my dad were friends in college. Amazing, huh? When you read my story, you'll understand why I can't present it."

When we get to the cabin, I ask Olive to wait outside until I confirm everyone is decent. The three guys are on their beds, putting the finishing touches on their work for the finals.

"Yo, my girlfriend's here. Can I bring her in?"

"Sure," Luke says. They all stop what they're doing, even Malik, who usually never pauses his writing for anyone, but I guess a girl in our room is a big deal.

I introduce her to the bros. "This is Olive." I point at each one of them in turn and say, "This is Yoshiki and his brother, Luke. They're both artists."

"Hi, guys." Olive doesn't blink at how different these brothers look.

"And you already met Malik."

Malik stands and soaks in Olive's stares. Bringing her here might have been a serious mistake. In comparison to Malik, I look like a bowl of oatmeal. She's in his spell like all the other girls.

I get my story out of the folder and hand it to Olive. "Read this."

Malik gives her his million-dollar smile and offers her a spot on the bed. I don't like that arrangement, but there aren't any chairs in the room. He continues to flash his pearly whites and then sits right next to her. All summer he ignores the girls, and now he has the time to focus on Olive. What's up with that, buddy?

While she's reading, I prepare the guys. "I may not stay for the awards because I have to go to a wedding. I'm the best man." This excuse seems plausible because every good lie should have a bit of truth in it to make it believable. For the first time since Mom's big announcement, the word wedding streams out of my mouth without hitching at the back of my throat.

Yosh laughs. "You as a best man? Doubtful. Who would ask you?"

"It's true. Ted and my mom are getting married, and they did ask me."

Luke's smile turns smirky. "Hah! And you tried to pass him off as just a friend. I guess he's a very, very good friend. Congrats on the new type of father."

Yosh gives me an exploding fist bump, and Luke comes

down from his top bunk to bear-hug me. His yucky sweat rubs off on my face, but I ignore that this time.

I glance at Malik, who's riveted on Olive as she reads my story. When she finishes, she raises her eyes from the paper and proclaims, "You rock, Rocky. You did it. You wrote a story that slices and dices Ted."

She hands me the papers, and I rip them in half.

Malik jumps up and grabs the two halves from me. "Don't do that!"

"I was in a grim place when I wrote this. This story would crush my mom. Ted is no longer the boogie man who is persecuting me. This story can never find the light of day."

"But you have to keep it," Malik says. "Never throw out something you've written. You can rework it or use parts of it in a different story." He reacts as if I'm about to tear up a thousand dollar bill and flush it down the toilet, but I guess he's got a point. I put the torn papers in my folder.

"You must have another story you can read tomorrow," Malik says.

"But I worked hard on this new story, and it was so good."

"You could read the one about the talking bird," Olive suggests.

"Oh, the bird. How did you remember that one?" I ask her, flipping through my old notebook to find it. Good old Sylvester, my Uber-flying bird.

"I never forget a thing, Rockala."

"I'll have to do some revising before tomorrow," I say.

"Well, then get busy," Malik says. "I'm done with my work. I'll walk Olive back up."

Ugh.

THE NEXT MORNING, Luke is in nonstop-babble mode because he's tense on this day of judgment for all of us. Malik puts on his lucky shoes. So much has happened in three weeks. I'm excited but also so ready to go home.

The log cabin is festive with blue and gold streamers hanging from the rafters and bunches of balloons in each corner. Above the podium there's a gigantic sign that reads Lakeside Program for the Arts and Writing. Someone is standing in the back of the hall behind a tripod with a video camera to preserve this event forever.

Mom and Ted are chatting with Ms. Simmons. I find Olive sitting on a bench studying her phone.

"Hey, Olive, how did you like being my mom's roommate last night? Hope she didn't snore." I expect a wisecrack in return, and when there is none, I notice her eyes glistening but not in a sparkly way. She squeezes them once or twice, which is a sure sign she's holding back tears.

"Are you okay?" I ask her as Althea comes to the mike and urges everyone to take their seats.

Olive says, "Got a text. There's something wrong at home. I sense it. Mom said there's an important family dinner as soon as I get back. My spidey sense tells me it's bad news."

I've had my own experience with big announcements I wished I never heard. I give Olive some of her own excellent advice and say, "Maybe it isn't anything bad. Sometimes our minds go haywire and we head down roads we shouldn't be traveling. I've done that a few too many times. Your family dinner might be wonderful."

Her face brightens a little when Mom and Ted sit next to her. Mom pats Olive's hand, which could be nothing or could be a sign she knows something is wrong in Olive's family.

"Later," I say and take my seat.

This time Althea calls up Malik to read his work before me, and his story is nothing short of amazing. No way he won't win. I'll have to wait to get to Los Angeles. My dad will understand. I hope Malik's dad loves the trip.

At last, it's my turn to take my shot. I gaze out at the audience and lock eyes on my three fans. Mom seems nervous, Olive sends me a double thumbs-up, and Ted looks gleeful, with his crazy eyebrows in a full range of motion.

I read my bird story:

A sudden whoosh of cold air blows into my room, and I push against the forceful wind to close the window. Hovering outside is a rather large bird similar to an eagle with shiny black wing feathers, eyes the color of tar, and a red tuft of feathers sticking up on top of its head.

"Joe," the bird chirps with a warm, melty marshmallow voice. "Climb aboard."

I'm freaked. This talking bird is inviting me for a ride.

"Where to?" I ask.

"Somewhere special. I'm your Uber flying bird."

"Did my mother send you?"

"No. I'm flying you to freedom," the bird says.

This doesn't sound right, but then again, a chance to ride a bird isn't something you're offered every day. I put on my gray hoodie in case he flies into colder air and stuff my phone in my pocket, because I'm def going to need a selfie of this.

As I lift my leg to climb out of the window, my bedroom door bangs open, and Mom skids as if the floor is slippery, lands on her belly and slides toward me. She grabs my legs.

"Where are you going?" Her voice is high-pitched like a wounded animal whose lifeblood is oozing out. It hurts my ears to listen to her.

"Just for a ride."

She squeezes tight, cutting off the blood flow to my feet which are now numb.

The bird's voice transforms from smooth and sweet to raspy and angry, "Joe's mother, let him go," he orders. The bird's beak grows into a dagger-like point and the tuft of red becomes a wild mess of feathers, pointing in every direction. The bird doesn't appear so harmless now.

"Never," Mom replies.

I jump up and down a few times to loosen her grip, and as soon as I'm free, I dash toward the window.

"Sorry, Mom, this is a once in a lifetime opportunity."

"Stay here with me," she whimpers.

I lift my eyes for a sec to check how Mom is reacting to Joe's mom. She's smiling, so that's good. Moms always want to be with their kids. That's a no-brainer. I continue to read.

The bird slows its wings almost to a stop, making it safer to climb aboard. How it stays aloft is a mystery.

I lie face down on the bird's back and grab on to a clump of feathers, being extra careful not to hold too tightly in case I accidentally yank one out. That might be as painful as pulling off a person's fingernail. Youch!!

"Are you ready?" the bird asks, after I stop wiggling around getting settled.

"Ready." I look back at the window. Mom's leaning out, waving frantically.

"Be safe," she shouts. "I'll miss you."

Mom knows I have to go, but I'm too scared to let go and wave, so I yell, "I'll miss you too."

And we're off! The bird flies at a steady clip. After a while, I'm brave enough to lift my head for a look around. First, we're over a dense forest that covers the ground with multi-shades of green treetops. Then we pass a lake which sparkles as if it's full of diamonds chunks. A city comes into view.

The bird turns halfway to glimpse me out of one eye. "Almost there," he says.

"Almost where?" I ask.

"To fix your chip problem so you can neutralize your mom."

"You're kidding."

"Isn't that what you really want?" the bird asks. "All kids want that."

I never thought that was even possible. Years ago, people would've called my mom a helicopter parent, but in 2052, she's known as a chip-parent, and I'm a chip-kid. Once I asked Mom why she agreed to get chipped.

She said, "Because I love you."

"You mean other kids' parents don't love them?" I responded.

Then she said, "It's because I want to be sure you're safe at all times."

She sees dangers lurking everywhere.

The bird lands on the sidewalk in front of a wooden shack wedged between clusters of tall shiny glass and steel structures. It has been decades since people built with wood. Trees are considered too precious. I slide off the bird's back.

After looking around, I'm ready to go home, but the bird is gone. He left me alone in this strange place. I send Mom a telepathic message through my chip to come get me. I wait, but she doesn't come. Usually, all I have to do is think I need her, and there she is. It's something I count on. The signal must be jammed. I have to go inside and ask whoever lives here to call her on his cyberpad.

I raise my fist to knock just as the door swings open. I step inside, and a strong sour smell bombards my nostrils. I try not to inhale until I have to gasp for air. An old man is stirring something in an electric pot. If he offers me a taste, my answer will be a loud no.

"I've been waiting for you, Joe," he says. "You want to unchip your mother?"

"No, I want to call her to pick me up."

"No cyber service here, and your chip is automatically uncoupled in this zone, so she has no idea where you are. You are free here."

Another time, that might have sent me into a happy dance, but not now while I'm in this strange place where Mom may never find me. I lift the end of my T-shirt and dab my eyes.

"Relax, kid. I'm going to teach you how to disconnect your mother's chip so she won't follow your every move. Then Sylvester will return and take you home."

"The...uh...bird?" I ask.

"Yes, of course. Sylvester, the bird."

"First, you must take an oath never to share what you learn here. If you do, bad juju will rain down on your family."

"I swear I won't tell a soul." If this guy shows me how to do anything that's going to hurt my mom, I will not do it.

He spreads out some blueprint drawings and then places a detached arm on the table. I'm assuming this came out of a 3-D printer and not off a real body. Yucko.

He strokes his beard and tucks it to the side out of his way. He lifts the "skin" on the arm and proceeds to explain technical stuff. I nod, pretending to follow his mumble-jumble. The arm even oozes fake blood when he presses it in certain spots. He reaches for a dirty rag, wipes up the liquid, and stuffs the damp, disgusting cloth into his pocket. I have to swallow down some rising barf.

"Look here," he says, pointing to a rectangular piece of

metal in the arm right under the surface. "This is the chip parents insert to monitor their kids. All you have to do to disengage it is to press it in the lower left corner three times."

Ha. Am I supposed to ask Mom to let me press her chip? I smile at this guy's foolish notion.

Then, as if he's reading my inner thoughts, he says, "You have to be subtle when you do this. Some kids cannot do subtle no matter how much they practice."

"I can do it."

"While giving your mother a hug, you put one hand on her chipped arm and quickly press the corner of the elevated part. You can't miss the spot if you know what you're looking for. It's as easy as that."

He makes me practice a few times on the fake arm, and then when he's satisfied, he pushes me out the door. No goodbye, no nothing, and I'm back on the sidewalk. The bird is already there, perched on the bottom step.

"Are you going to bring me home?" I ask, unsure if he has other plans for me.

"Yes."

"Promise you will take me straight to my house. No stops along the way."

He cackles and with each caw spits droplets of saliva. I move a few steps away to avoid getting it on me.

I have to pause because everyone's laughing at the bird spit part. Once it's quiet, I finish the story.

"I promise, now climb on."

I have no choice. I get situated quickly, and we head for the skies, flying above puffy clouds that rarely break to show the earth below. In a short time, the bird is in front of my bedroom window. I scramble inside.

Within a second, Mom is there. Her chip must've alerted her I'm back. She hugs me, and slowly I lift my hand and place it on her arm.

The End

I sit down.

PART 5:

HOME IN MILTON

CHAPTER 35

One last check in the mirror to admire some authentic high school material. Me! My cell rings. It's too awkward to answer a Facetime call in the bathroom, so I scurry back to my room.

Malik's face appears, beaming his too-good-to-be-true grin. "Hey, just checking in."

"How do you like my new jacket?" I ask as I move the phone down so Malik gets the full view of this bold green, blue, and pink plaid.

"Not bad for a soccer player," he laughs.

I lower the cell phone even further to show off my red Nike slides.

"You've got some style," he says.

"Thanks." Ted and I went shopping for wedding duds, and he agreed that a guy who's almost fourteen should be allowed to have his own taste. I can't wait to pop a selfie of this splendor on Instagram.

"You'll never guess where I am," Malik says. "We're in the stadium waiting for the game between the Red Sox and the L.A. Dodgers to start. I know who you're rooting for."

"Sox all the way," I say and pump my fist in the air.

"There's someone here who wants to say hi." Malik's dad

moves into the picture, and he flings his arm around Malik, which makes Malik's smile grow even bigger, as if he ate a bucket of happy beans.

His dad says, "Thank you for saving my boy. I hope I can meet you sometime. Malik suggests we take a road trip to Milton to watch one of your soccer games. He mentioned something about soccer players riding horses, but he's got his sports mixed up."

I try not to laugh, which is almost impossible when I picture myself holding the reins with my big goalie gloves. Malik better acknowledge me in the credits for that story because I'm the person who gave him the idea.

"Great. Come anytime. I'll text Malik the schedule of my home games. I've got to go. My mom's wedding is about to start." Whatever jealousy I had once about Malik is gone. When he won the award, I cheered louder than anyone, and now he's in Los Angeles with his dad.

"Be cool," Malik says.

"I'm always cool. I learned coolness from one of the best."

Malik laughs.

I fly downstairs, almost knocking over Ted, who's waiting at the bottom for me.

"You look great, Rocky." He hands me a tiny box. "Hang on tight to these. The minister will give you the signal when it's time to give him the rings."

"Where's Mom?" I ask, putting the ring box in my top jacket pocket.

"She's holed up in her room getting ready with her BFF. Rochelle came over early so they'd have hours for whatever it is they're doing up there."

We both laugh, and I notice his little beard is gone, and he has trimmed those wild, massive eyebrows. That is a major improvement. I guess he's making a fresh start on his wedding day.

I leave him to check in on Grandpa, who's in his chair as usual, but not reading.

"No book, Grandpa?" I ask.

"Today is a thinking day," he says. "I'm trying to savor it all. Your mom's thrilled. You seem good, too. Makes me happy."

"Yup, I'm on board. Bought a ticket to ride this marriage train with them."

He stands up without grimacing in pain and wraps me in his arms.

When I remember my resistance to Ted and the whole marriage idea, I shudder. Another kid might have handled it better, but I had convinced myself that my supply of life adjustments had run out, and I couldn't handle one more change. I was wrong. Life always changes. Sometimes in not such good ways, and sometimes in okay ways. Life isn't like treading water. You have to keep moving and swim with the current, but when the water gets choppy, you work twice as hard to get where you want to go, but it's totally worth it.

📄

AN AWNING COVERS the backyard so we don't bake. There are flowers everywhere and even an archway of roses for Mom to walk under when the ceremony begins. Off to the side, a man and a woman play violin and flute duets. It isn't rock or hip-hop, but they're mellow and have a joyful vibe.

Olive, Max, and Madison are already here. I join them and lean in close to Max to check that he showered off any telltale baby brother scent. He's fine.

Olive gasps and runs her eyes from my hair to my bare feet

in the red slides. "Rocking the new duds. Do you have a personal dresser now, Rocky?"

"Ha. No. I just have flair. I'm making a statement in more ways than one. After all, I'm the best man. I don't plan to fade into the background today."

"Oh. Oh. What are you cooking up? I love your mom. You'd better not embarrass her at her wedding," Olive warns.

"Wait and see," I say, keeping the big reveal even from her.

Since we got back from Lakeside, Olive's going through a rough patch because she found out her parents are having problems, and her usual sarcasm and funny comments have become casualties as a result. She told me, "Now, I'm the one who's living in Trouble City." That's a destination no one wants to visit.

Mostly, Olive tries to pretend everything will turn out fine with her family, but I'm not sure she's convinced herself. I hope being at Mom's wedding doesn't make her extra sad about her parents.

Ted comes over with a line of people trailing him. He introduces me to his sister, brother-in-law, and their two kids. Jeanie looks like the woman in the photo I found in his wallet, which is a sore reminder of me breaking into Ted's private stuff. I'm lucky he has forgiven me.

When they leave, Olive returns to the previous subject. "Rocky, not sure what you have in mind when you say you won't fade into the background today, but no funny business."

"Don't you trust me?" I ask with a mischievous grin.

"I'm not sure," she replies.

Max grabs a mini pizza from a waiter's tray to add to his handful of hot-dogs-in-blankets. He must've snagged at least a dozen of those.

"Hey, slow down, man, there'll be more food later." I offer advice that's unwelcome to a kid who is never not hungry.

Madison has Velcroed herself to Max, convinced they're boyfriend and girlfriend, but I'm not sure if Max has signed on to that arrangement yet. He should. She's great.

The minister takes his place, and Ted taps me on the shoulder, which means it's time. He walks toward the minister and stands next to him. I go into the house and wait for Mom.

The music changes, and Mom joins me, wearing her extraordinary smile. I cringe, thinking I almost prevented this day from happening. She loops her arm under mine and leans over to peck me on the cheek. The sweet smell of a large white flower above her ear is better than any perfume. We stand side by side, and I savor finally being taller than she is. I touch my pocket one more time to make sure the rings are there. We walk slowly. Very slowly.

Everyone stands and gawks at Mom. She's so beautiful. When we get to the minister, I move to the other side so she's standing between Ted and me. When the minster asks for the rings, I put them both in his hand. Before I know it, he's saying, "I now pronounce you husband and wife according to the laws of the Commonwealth of Massachusetts."

There's furious clapping when Ted kisses her, and it doesn't make me puke in the slightest. I've come a long way since I wanted to FedEx Ted to the other side of the world.

The two of them turn to greet the guests, and a photographer moves in to snap photos. Ted grabs me and pulls me into the picture right between them. I slam on a wicked smile powerful enough to dominate the photo and hope the photographer's shot includes my fantastic red slides.

When I'm free, I hustle over to my friends and ask, "So, guys, was it too mushy?"

Max rolls his eyes.

Madison's in a trance and says, "Are you kidding? It was amazing." She gazes at Max and adds, "Ooo, the kiss." Max responds by making fifth-grade kissing noises into the air. What a guy.

Olive's smile is low-key. She whispers to me, "I wish my dad was kissing my mom like that." Before I can say anything to cheer her up, Mom and Ted haul me off to the kitchen for a meeting.

Inside, Mom takes both my hands and says, "Rocky, Ted and I want you to be part of everything, so the three of us will honeymoon together in Orlando."

Ted gives me a sidelong glance. I keep my word not to let on I already know about the honeymoon-for-all idea. I force my eyes wide and form my mouth into an enormous gaping hole to show my fake surprise and throw my arms around Mom, saying, "I can't believe you both would do that for me. It's gonna be awesome."

"Yes, it will," Ted says and gives me an enthusiastic pat on the back. I didn't blow it, and I kept him out of trouble.

"One more announcement," Mom says. "We're not moving. Ted is going to sell his house. You were right. Grandpa needs our help, and as a bonus, you can still walk to school."

Okay, this is officially a stupendous day in every way. I'm surprised Ted would do this for us, but maybe I shouldn't be after what I know about him now.

After all the guests are seated for the luncheon, I stand and clink my glass with a knife being careful not to send crunchy glass crystals flying onto people's plates.

Mom narrows her eyes until they almost meet at her nose, and her cheeks become bright pink. She's nervous because I never told her I planned to make a speech, but I googled best man, and the toast is an important part of my job.

"Today my family changes," I start. "It isn't the first time there have been changes for me, so you might think I'm a pro at this. I'm not. I was pretty much a brat about Mom getting married. It took me a while before I was willing to give Ted a chance.

"This summer I had a lesson in how families are different in many ways. Two of my roommates were brothers. They're the same age, but they're not twins, and no, this isn't a riddle. One of them is Japanese, and I don't know the background of the other guy, but he looks more like me than his brother Yoshiki. Of course, it all made sense when they told us Luke was adopted. I didn't expect Yosh's parents would choose a kid with blond hair and blue eyes to join their family.

"Another of my roommates has a dad with two sons from another marriage, and my friend was convinced his dad liked his older brothers better, but he was wrong. That kid won the top writing prize at Lakeside and is now in Los Angeles with his super-proud father, picking up his award.

"And now my family includes Ted."

Everyone clinks glasses and says, "Cheers." As I sit, I yank off my strangulation tie and shove it into my pocket. My best man responsibilities are over.

Olive gives me a double thumbs up, so I know I did good.

"Rocket Man, do you think you are finished with family changes?" she asks me.

"Yes. Mom's not marrying anyone else," I laugh.

"But maybe you'll become a member of Max's new baby barf club."

ROCKY'S STORY FOR THE FINAL PRESENTATION

DESTROY AFTER YOU READ IT!

The annoying AI-TABLET announces 7:00 with a series of beeps ascending in shrillness until I shout at it to shut up. There is no going back to sleep after that ear-attack.

I poke my head out the window. The sky is almost totally black and filled with a constant buzzing.

I reach for my noise-cancelling headphones to block the noise and wonder why people in the olden days thought we'd be better off closing all of the real stores and flooding the sky with hordes of drones until there wasn't a speck of blue or white clouds to be seen.

For the first day of eighth grade, I wear my shirt that says class of 2062 and order my breakfast. When I get to the Superkitch, my food is waiting. I sit on the stool and notice my feet almost touch the floor. Between seventh and eighth grade, I grew a lot as my DNA chart predicted. I'm closing in on six feet which makes me happy.

On my way out, I open the door to Mom's office. She looks up and says, "This is going to be a special day for you."

"Special?" I ask.

"Special with lots of surprises," she replies and goes back to her GoogZoom with a client.

I put my AI-TAB into my crossbody bag and grab my hoverboard. I glide on the special path to Astro Middle where I join throngs of kids pouring in through automatic steel doors that block wayward drones and people who don't have proper facial recognition on file.

Once inside the building, I park my hoverboard against the wall and tap my ID card to lock it. I glance at my schedule. First period is current events, but the teacher is TBD. I ask the tablet who TBD is, and the answer is "you'll find out." Pretty snarky, AI.

In the classroom, the teacher is scuzzy with wild hair and a gruesome beard, though he could easily go into the bathroom and request a quick fix-up from the groom-robot. There's no excuse nowadays for someone to walk around like that, but perhaps I shouldn't judge him only by his appearance. Still, this dude looks weird.

"Greetings. I am Teacher-DET. Welcome to current events. This class will change your life. I guarantee it."

I detect from his accent that he isn't from Earth. Why did they hire an alien to teach us?

"Turn your tablets to today's lecture about recent discoveries in the solar system."

I know this stuff cold.

Teacher-DET asks, "Who can identify the newest galaxy?" My hand shoots up, and he calls on me.

I can't control my smirky face, as I say, "Plutek's Orbs." As soon as those words are spoken, my mouth slams shut. That's completely wrong. The right answer is trapped in my throat, but I can't cough it up.

"Wrong, Titan. Sirius, do you know the name?"

Sirius never knows anything.

"Satanus," he answers. And then whispers to me, "It's so obvious."

And he's so obnoxious.

"That's correct. Well done, Sirius," Teacher-DET says.

Something strange just happened. For the rest of the class, Teacher-DET talks about star clusters and then gives us a pop quiz. A quiz on the first day is evil.

By lunchtime, I'm still shaken by the morning's blunder. In the Automat-Cafe, I watch the slideshow of today's choices whiz by and touch the screen to make my selections. My mom tells me how she had to carry a tray through a line when she was my age. People were so funny back then.

By the time I get to my table, my food is there, but it's not what I ordered. For the first time ever at Astro Middle, they messed up my lunch. I have a plate of soupy green food with pieces of brown I-don't-know-what floating in it. I can't even look at it. I wait for my friends to show up and hope they'll have something to share.

But instead of any kids, Teacher-DET sits down. "The triple green special. I ordered it for you. You'll love it." Then he hands me my quiz.

I failed. I never fail. I'm one of the top eighth graders in the school.

"I am assigning my personal robot to tutor you. It will never leave your side."

"I don't need that. I'll do better," I promise.

"My robot is top of the line, a 2060 XXXX edition." His eyes flicker as if they're sending a message, and all of a sudden a robot about as high as the table appears. Now everyone will know I'm in trouble and that I need robot-help. Teacher-DET leaves, but my friends never show up. For the first time, I have to sit totally alone at lunch and leave the cafeteria confused, upset, and starving.

The rest of the classes drag, and I'm anxious to get to soccer to distract me from this disaster of a day.

In the locker room, there's a big commotion on the other side of the row of lockers. I walk over to check it out, and there is Teacher-DET chatting up the players as if he's a magnetic force, and they're made out of iron.

He sees me. "Hi, Titan."

"Hi, Teacher-DET."

"At soccer, call me Coach-DET."

My heart skips a few beats. This guy is everywhere.

I change and put on my yellow goalie gloves. I'm the Astro's permanent goalie, and we've made the playoffs ever since I've been in that position. I station myself in front of the net. At the half, the score is lopsided with the New Moons ten and the Astros a big fat zero. I've been playing soccer since small peeps teams in elementary school, and I've never let in so many goals.

DET, I mean Coach-DET, announces that he's putting Sirius in as goalie from now on. I'm not just benched, but replaced. He makes me ball boy, the kid who chases the balls that go off the field. Humiliating.

I'm a jumble of raw energy as I watch Astro's offense on fire, unlike their dull first half, and they pull out a victory I was not a part of. The final score is 11 to 10.

I change my clothes fast, grab my hoverboard and head home, dejected. I can't understand what happened to me today. It's like someone cast an evil spell on me. As soon as I get home, I'll have to immerse myself in the decompression chamber.

I stare at my front door's recognition unit, waiting for it to open. Inside, Mom calls out, "There are cookies just out of the oven."

My nose leads me to the warm, chocolatey scent in the Superkitch. When Mom sees me, her eyes bulge out of their sockets and practically wallop me in the face.

"You're so pale. Let me check you out."

I know the drill and follow her to the exam room. She puts the Temp-Oxygen-Squeezer on my right index finger and a band on my forehead which measures brain waves. Then she touches the tiny port on my arm and takes a drop of blood to put it in the Rapid Analyzer. Now that everyone has one of these rooms at home, only the worst cases have to go to a doctor.

Mom reads the screens in front of her and says, "Well, physically you're fine so it must be psychological. Did something special happen at school?"

"No," I answer, because at thirteen you don't go crying to your mommy.

"Well, something special is happening here today. I'm getting married. The man will be here soon. You'll love him."

"So suddenly?"

"Yes. Sudden is best for these types of changes."

The AI-TAB announces someone's at the door. Mom instructs the door to open.

"Hi, Titan."

My mouth drops open in shock. "Coach-DET!" I scream in horror.

"Here at home you can call me Daddy-DET. I'm going to be in your life forever and make sure you have more days just like today."

Mom has brought the enemy into our home.

The End

ACKNOWLEDGMENTS

The acknowledgement pages at the end of a book are a gift from the publisher to allow an author space to thank the many people who share in bringing a book into the world.

Before I thank the "real" people, I must mention Rocky. I love that boy! I had no intention of writing a sequel to my debut middle grade mystery, Swallowed by a Secret, but when I started a new story, Rocky wouldn't leave center stage and demanded, once again, to be front and center as the main character.

I'm so lucky to be part of an extraordinary publishing family–Immortal Works. Everything begins with Staci Olsen, my acquisitions editor and the production manager who shepherds new books on their road to publication. There is nothing better than receiving an email from Staci with an offer for a contract. Without her, I wouldn't be writing these acknowledgments.

There are many others at Immortal Works who deserve thanks, especially Chief Editor Holli Anderson. I also want to mention two former IW staff members who were always so supportive and helpful and have my deep appreciation – Rachel Huffmire, former Marketing Manager, and Beth Buck, former Acquisitions Director.

Also, kudos to Ashley Literski, the Creative Manager at Immortal Works, for the outstanding cover design and to my editor, Audrey Hammer for her thoughtful comments and edits on the manuscript.

I am grateful to the awesome and talented Immortal Works authors who I have met online and appreciate their willingness to share their knowledge and best practices and to provide encouragement whenever needed.

Thank you to the Inked Voices website, my writing village. This is where I participate in workshops led by the amazing author Jen Malone and share my work with exceptional critique partners who read and reread these chapters and improve my story and my writing. My heartfelt thanks to Steve Arnold, Jacquelyn Carberry, Kristine Carter, Heidi Casper, Kim Holster, and Patricia Nesbitt.

Rawles Lumumba, a professional editor and sensitivity reader, reviewed this manuscript on issues of diversity for appropriateness and accuracy. Her insights were invaluable.

A special acknowledgment to Lisa Stringfellow, a gifted author, who is so generous in her support. It is an honor to call her friend.

Many dear friends join me on my writing adventure and are cherished cheerleaders. My deepest thanks to: Ina Tamir, Alvene Williams, Karen Kavet, Nancy Carapezza, Linda and Jerry Benezra, Becky and Andy Ceperley, Annette Needle and Peter Meyersohn, and Carole Wagner Vallianos and Pete Vallianos. I appreciate the steadfast support of my brother and sister-in-law, Leonard and Lois Sharzer.

I want to thank three special people who are always there for me – David Malkiel, Mark Chapin, and Ben Reiss.

A big shoutout to the jewels of my life – my grandchildren.

This book is dedicated to my cherished daughters who are my world.

And as people have a penchant to do, I close with the best of the best, my beloved Philip who is always steadfastly beside me.

ABOUT THE AUTHOR

Born in Boston with the accent to prove it, Risa lived within ten miles of that city for decades until a recent move to the neighboring Ocean State.

For many years, Risa worked in a nonpartisan, not-for-profit organization dedicated to promoting active participation in our democracy, with a special focus on voting and elections.

Risa's creative writing journey started the day she found three pennies in a neat stack on a windowsill in a completely empty apartment that had belonged to her mother. It's an interesting story, and there was definitely some magic in those pennies.

When not writing, Risa is reading, exercising or doing therapeutic ironing (yes, there is such a thing.)

This has been an
Immortal Production

CPSIA information can be obtained
at www.ICGtesting.com
Printed in the USA
BVHW032222160821
614594BV00006B/179

9 781953 491213